cabin
clearing
forest

CABIN, CLEARING, FOREST

Zach Falcon

UNIVERSITY OF ALASKA PRESS, FAIRBANKS

Text © 2015 University of Alaska Press
All rights reserved

University of Alaska Press
PO Box 756240
Fairbanks, AK 99775-6240

Library of Congress Cataloging-in-Publication Data

Falcon, Zach.
    [Short Stories. Selections]
    Cabin, clearing, forest / by Zach Falcon.
      p. cm
    ISBN 978-1-60223-275-4 (pbk. : alk. paper)
    ISBN 978-1-60223-276-1 (e-book)
    I. Title.
    PS3606.A4235A6 2016
    813'.6--dc23

                          2014049540

Cover and interior design by Jen Gunderson, 590 Design LLC
Cover image Aleksandra Kovac

This publication was printed on acid-free paper that meets the minimum
requirements for ANSI / NISO Z39.48–1992 (R2002) (Permanence of Paper for
Printed Library Materials).

for K.A.C.

You won't find a new country, won't find another shore.
This city will always pursue you.

C.P. Cavafy, *The City*

cabin

THERE ARE NO SECRETS IN SMALL HOUSES. The children, Mark and Hazel, knew things were wrong long before their parents admitted it. Before the seething quiet, before their father started sleeping on the couch, before their mother's humor boiled away, leaving her reduced, thick, and bitter.

A sticky patch divided the table between them. A smear of Mark's jam, or maybe Hazel's syrup. The children had pancakes that morning, wolfing them down and running outside like feral cats. Bruce's arm bent at an odd angle to avoid the spot as he reached across the table to touch Ellen's hand. "Everything is okay," he said.

1

Ellen stared at the mole on Bruce's arm. It had never bothered her before, but now it seemed sinister, like a sign of underlying pollution become manifest. A message she had ignored.

"Everything is okay," he repeated, touching her fingers, cold and still.

She stared at the mole. The hair on Bruce's arm was coarser around it. They heard Mark's stomp on the porch, heavy for such a small boy, and Ellen startled. Mark pushed open the front door a crack and shouted, "We're gonna ride bikes." He closed the door and stomped away.

Bruce clasped her hand and pulled it closer, sweeping Ellen's arm into the sticky spot. She jerked away sharply and rubbed at the smear on her elbow, tipping her head to listen for the children outside.

"They don't know," Bruce said. "They didn't even notice."

Ellen met his eyes. "And that's all that matters?" she asked flatly.

It began in the summer, the secretive dour restlessness of their parents, so the children spent as much time outside as possible. They probably would have done so anyway but for the animal shadow always outside, lurking. The children avoided the bad luck of speaking about it aloud. They never mentioned him to their parents. Without saying so, they agreed that the risk he presented was preferable to being inside.

Hazel was nine, Mark six. They both had bicycles. Hazel's bicycle was a Miss America model: pink frame, pink banana seat, red, white, and blue streamers hanging from the handle grips. Mark rode a black-and-yellow Huffy. The Huffy did not have a motif, superhero or otherwise, but Mark had given it a secret name and valued it highly.

Mark, riding alone, would turn endless wobbling circles without leaving the gravel driveway. But Hazel was adventurous and led him farther afield. They followed a circuit: first coasting down the driveway until they were hidden from their house by the dense forest and then pedaling furiously to the first turn at the bottom of the hill. Right led past their few neighbors and up to the paved road into town. Left led onto the back road that wound into the state park before becoming a trail and ending at the sea. They almost always turned left.

Ellen took an early afternoon nap. Even so, Bruce kept his voice low when he called Cherise. "No," he whispered. "I can't see you today." The phone was mounted to the wall by the front door, next to the window. Bruce's breath steamed the pane as he listened, staring out into the tangled forest surrounding their house. "No. I said I can't. It's impossible." He lifted a finger and drew the shape of a cabin in the steam and then drew a circle close around it. "I don't know." He made a fist and wiped the doodle away with the flesh of his compressed palm. "Well," he said, glancing back at the door closed between him and his wife, "maybe for just a bit, if it's soon." Through the window he saw a dark shape moving through the forest. Reddish brown, a flash of white. Not a bear. He couldn't make it out, and it flickered back into shadow. "Okay," he said. He hung up, setting the phone back carefully, as though defusing a bomb.

The bedroom door opened and Ellen stumbled out. "You son-ofabitch," she said, pointing. "You weren't gonna." Her face was flushed and her hair was flattened and matted with spit on one side. "You weren't gonna."

Bruce turned away from her, pulling on his boots, grabbing his jacket, opening the door. "You're drunk," he said, closing the door behind him.

They left their bikes where the narrow trail became too knotted with twisting bulks of spruce root to ride any farther. Hazel walked ahead while Mark dawdled, picking salmonberries and eating them from the bushes without checking for worms. "Gross," said Hazel. "The worms will crawl out through your skin." Mark shrugged. His nose ran and he sniffed loudly, licking his upper lip. "Gross," repeated Hazel, striding well ahead. Through the trees they could hear the ocean heave against the black-rock beach below the distant cliffs, and then ebb, sucking between the barnacles like teeth.

"Haze?" said Mark, suddenly anxious. Something massive moved in the thicket of devil's club beyond, snapping branches. The heavy rub of an animal threading through the brush. "Hey, Haze, wait up."

She stopped. "Well c'mon then." He ran to her, dropping the salmonberries from his hand.

They followed the main trail, ignoring its looping side branches that led nowhere in particular, until it opened free of the forest and ended at the crest of a bluff above Mill Bay. The surf broke high and white on the rocks below them. On the promontory sat a small cement-walled pillbox, a derelict bunker left from the island's World War II defenses. The dank inside was cluttered with beer cans, junk food wrappers, and an inexplicable single, laceless leather boot. A stained mattress slumped in a corner. The mildewed walls dripped with wet. Mark and Hazel peered through the gaping doorway to see if anything had changed and then climbed to the roof, which was carpeted with soft emerald moss and sprouting grass. They avoided the sagging middle and stood on the firm front edge. Behind them pressed the forest and before them spread the North Pacific, the gray roilings of the Gulf of Alaska. "From here we can see everything," said Hazel, waving her arms at the curving horizon as though she had created everything by magic herself alone. She always said it, and Mark always nodded, though it didn't seem that they could see anything at all.

Bruce drove to town but stopped only to get gas and call Cherise to cancel from the station's crusted payphone. Denny Martin stood at the other pump, and they nodded as the gas clicked in. "How's the family?" asked Denny. "Good, good," said Bruce, nodding. He paid for the gas and bought a pack of gum and a bottle of brown soda. He set the bottle on the bench seat and unwrapped the foil from five sticks of gum. He chewed them together like it was his job, until his jaw groaned and popped from the effort. Driving back the two miles along the coast he could have seen his children atop the pillbox if he was looking, if he could have seen so far.

Bruce parked the truck and stalked through their small house with a black garbage bag, hunting for hidden bottles and dropping them each with a clink into the rustling plastic. He wet a washcloth with warm water and took it together with the soda into the bedroom where Ellen still lay diminished in the tangled blankets. He sat on the bed and wiped her face, brushing back the stray wet hairs, tucking them behind her ears. "I ended it," he said. "It's over." He opened the hissing soda and she raised her head to drink.

"And that's all that matters?" she repeated.

Mark built a house out of twigs on the roof of the pillbox until Hazel grew restless and wanted to move on. Crawling down from the roof was trickier than climbing up to it. They lowered themselves backward, sliding their bellies tight against the black slime of the cement wall, until their feet touched a low shelf-like outcropping of the building. Hazel went first and then guided Mark down, holding his legs. They brushed absently at their clothes, but the slime left wet smears that stained.

They followed the trail back to where they had left their bikes. Hazel noticed the green leaves of a twisted stalk plant, and they knelt to eat its watery berries that tasted vaguely like melon. The flat gray sky above them, barely visible beneath the arching colander of spruce trees, began to drizzle, and the air turned cold and quiet. Mark sniffled and caught a scurrying ground beetle in his palm, showing it to Hazel who nodded gravely. When they had eaten all the ripe berries, they stood and wandered easily down the trail, through the tunneled dimness of the forest toward the road.

"You know," said Hazel as they approached their bikes, "if you carve something into an apple tree, and then eat one of the apples, that thing will happen to you."

"What sort of something?" asked Mark.

"Anything. A wish. Everything."

"Oh," said Mark. "We don't have any apple trees here."

"I know," said Hazel.

"What about other trees?" Mark pointed into the forest.

"They're no good," said Hazel, shaking her head.

"What about salmonberries?" Mark persisted.

"Salmonberries just grow," said Hazel. "They don't mean anything."

Hazel walked ahead a few steps, but Mark had stopped. She turned and saw him staring into the forest. He stood transfixed and pale.

"What?" Hazel asked. "What is it?"

"There," croaked Mark. He could see the shape not twenty feet away, the rust-colored fur, the huge head with curving horns, the rolling black eyes gazing back at him. The figure seemed unreal until it made a sound like a moaning cough ending in an explosive snort.

Hazel shouted, snatching at Mark's arm before turning and racing down the trail. Mark followed, and they ran like chased ducks, shrieking. The young bull ambled out of the bracken and stepped onto the trail. It trotted behind the children, its skin rippling with the easy movement.

Hazel reached her bike first. She slung her leg over the seat as she lifted it from the ground and was pedaling before Mark had even made it to the road. He gripped the handlebars of his Huffy and pushed it a few steps to gather speed before jumping on. Behind them, the bull's trot shifted into a canter. He charged out of the forest and onto the road, pounding the dirt beneath him, closing the distance to Mark. Mark's jump onto the seat of his bicycle set the machine wobbling and he lost control, pitching headfirst into the ditch beside the road as the animal thundered past. Hazel pedaled ahead, outdistancing the bull. It abandoned his sprint and stood triumphant and snorting in the road for a moment before turning back into the forest and vanishing into the murk.

When the bull was gone, Hazel looped back and helped Mark untangle himself from his bike. He was scraped and crying and muddy, more shaken than wounded. Hazel brushed him off and soothed him. He left his bike in the ditch and walked stiffly with Hazel as she pushed her bike alongside. After a time he mastered his breathing and the ragged sobs subsided. They didn't speak.

Bruce stood on the porch, dumping the clanking garbage bag of bottles into the trash barrel when Mark and Hazel came up the drive. He watched them, his bedraggled children, soaked and dirty and distant from him. He called to Mark. "Where's your bike?" Mark shrugged. "Hazel, where's his bike?" His daughter looked at her brother nervously. "Where's his bike?" Bruce repeated.

"We left it," said Hazel.

"Well then go back and get it," said Bruce. Mark looked startled and Hazel nodded. She leaned her bike against the woodpile and turned back down the driveway.

"No," said Bruce. "Mark has to go back and get his own bike. Not you." He focused on Mark, standing aimless and apart. "You go get your bike. You wanted a bike. You have to learn to take care of it. Okay?" Mark nodded slowly. "Don't just leave it somewhere to rust or get stolen." Mark nodded again but stood rooted. "Well hustle, or you'll miss dinner. Hazel, get inside and help your mother." Bruce waved his hand at her, beckoning impatiently. "You've been gone all day. Where the hell do you kids go?"

Hazel watched Mark shuffle back down the driveway into the tunnel of the trees and then stepped up onto the porch. "Nowhere," she said.

Walking back to the ditch Mark took small steps and breathed shallowly and hummed quietly. All of these things made him tiny, nearly invisible. But having to touch something, even his bike, was too much. He could not retrieve it. The action would expose him to every lurking thing. He stood unmoving, stuck. His stillness was a thin film, and the least movement through it to the physical world would shatter it, loudly. A three-toed woodpecker hammered on a dying spruce, slapping away the dry bark with blinking flicks of its head. The sound warped and echoed strangely in Mark's ears, as though he was listening from inside a locked room and someone was knocking to get in. His hands turned blue in the chill, but he could not move them even to put them inside his pockets. His breath slowed and his blood stilled. He stood on the road, staring blankly at his bike, in a hibernation of panic. The woodpecker moved to a tree above the ditch and knocked again. Mark startled, then turned and ran.

Hazel passed by the kitchen on her way to the bedroom she shared with Mark. She saw her mother's flushed and blurry face and did not pause to talk. She closed the bedroom door and squatted next to her bed. In a Tupperware bowl wedged behind her nightstand was a cache of stolen things that she kept for comfort: a yellow plastic lighter, a single turquoise earring, a leather key fob, a refrigerator magnet, a withered corsage. It also held food swiped from the pantry during the night. She crammed several stale saltine crackers into her mouth and chewed, catching the crumbs in her cupped hands. She threw the crumbs in a far corner and stashed the bowl away carefully, then sat on the bed, running her tongue around her teeth to clear away the clinging remnants of cracker, listening for any sound outside her door.

Ellen didn't hear the front door open over the roar of the faucet as she washed the dishes. It was the worst time of day, when she felt queasy and disjointed and at sea. Every task required the utmost concentration, lest she stumble, or drop, or spill, and call shame down upon herself. The oven's preheat light clicked off, and she dried her hands and saw that Mark had seated himself at the kitchen table. He sat with his hands in his lap, staring out the window at the darkening forest.

"Dinner's not for a while yet," she told him. He shrugged. She asked him where Hazel was, and he shrugged again. She opened four chicken pot pie boxes and slid the pies into the oven. "You can set the table," she said.

Mark slid off the chair and padded over to the silverware drawer.

"You get it?" Bruce's voice came from the other room. Mark looked blankly at Ellen and shook his head. "Did you get your bike?" Bruce repeated.

"He says no," said Ellen, shouting back, wincing.

Bruce stuck his head into the kitchen and glowered at Mark. "Why not?"

Mark shrugged and stared at the floor, picking at his jeans. "He can get it later," said Ellen. "I told him to help me with dinner." Ellen noticed for the first time Mark's smeared clothes, that his face was grubby with dirt and dried tears. "What happened to you?" she asked.

"I fell," said Mark. She examined his elbows, decided that the scrapes would heal on their own, and told him to go wash.

At dinner, Bruce sat at the head of the table, facing the picture window as Ellen skidded a hot pie on each plate in turn. Hazel picked the burnt edges of crust off of hers with a show of annoyance. Bruce noticed and began to scold her and then looked away, out the window. Mark kept silent. He had reached a decision and the effort of suppressing it left him unable to speak. He was going to say that he had been scared. That he couldn't get the bike because he was scared, but he could not form his mouth around the words. Ellen left the oven door ajar to add its dying heat to the cold room and sat down heavily.

Bruce stiffened. "What the hell is that?" he asked. He pointed out the window at a dark reddish shadow moving through the bushes. "That's the same thing I saw earlier," he said. Ellen and the children twisted in their seats to look. Mark gasped and Hazel started mumbling something under her breath.

"It's Hodge's bull," said Ellen. "It gets out sometimes. I've seen it in the yard, just wandering around."

"Those goddamn people," said Bruce. He pushed back from the table and strode to the phone. The Hodges shared their party line, and Bruce knew the number without looking. He dialed, breathing loud. He grunted as he waited for someone to pick up. "Hodge? This is Bruce Salter. Look, your goddamn bull was loose out in the woods today. It's in my yard right now. That's dangerous. I've got kids. You better tie that fucking thing up or I swear to god I'll shoot it myself. I'll cut out its sirloin and leave it to rot, you hear me?" He slammed the phone down and turned to his watching family. "He goddamn better," he said.

They ate in silence, each hunched over their gloomy pie, the meat parts soft and wet.

clearing

THE BOWERS WERE GONE FROM KODIAK FOR MOST OF JULY. Shortly after they returned they stood naked on their front lawn. Brian and Clare, Emily and Tess. They stood holding hands, silent and unclothed.

We gawked as we drove by. Traffic stopped. We stood in clumps across the street as the police came and covered them and separated them and hid them away. And we were relieved, because we wanted them to be covered and hidden. We gathered to gossip about it at the post office and Tony's Bar. We shifted on our stools, and we said that the cops should sort it out and that DFYS should sort it out. The Bowers had called these furies into their lives and would have to live with them. This was not our problem.

"It's not like they were hippies or anything," said Rod Vester, setting down his beer, wiping his mouth. "It's just weird." We set down our beers and agreed. It was weird. No one could have seen it coming.

Brian and Clare had moved to Alaska from Pennsylvania. They came willingly to our island of spruce trees and rain and canneries and bars. He taught fourth grade at our elementary school. Refrigerators throughout our town were decorated with the artwork of his students, our children. He coached the junior girls' basketball team.

He was a good teacher and admired for it. We were happy to have him in our town.

Clare was a volunteer at the museum. She had studied our past, and every summer she guided tourists through our small collection of artifacts, explaining the Aleut, Russian, and American footprints on the island. She handled our heirlooms with reverence. The masks, the lacquer boxes, the steel harpoon tips. She knew the history of Kodiak better than we did. She brought coffee to homeless Old Jacob Panamarioff when he sat carving on the bench outside the museum door. Old Jacob would smile for her, crinkling the weathered skin around his dark eyes. Tourists thought she was a local.

The Bowers bought the large white house on the hill downtown when Emily was born. Tess was born two years after. Brian painted a loud blue *B* on the front of the house, marking it as their home. They entertained often, and we were invited. The Bowers hosted a Fourth of July picnic on their lawn every year. Their house was on the paved road, so the parade passed right by. We would wave and catch the wrapped taffy thrown in fistfuls from the fire truck. The Bowers lived in Kodiak as publicly as a sidewalk tree.

The Fourth of July picnic at the Bowers' was cancelled this year. Clare's father had a heart attack at sixty-three. They traveled back to

Syracuse for the funeral, planning to spend only a week in the Lower 48 because Brian had a fishing trip scheduled on the Karluk and did not want to disappoint his companions. While they were in New York, Brian learned that his mother had suffered a stroke, so they traveled to Pennsylvania to be at her bedside.

Emily Bower had never met her grandmother. Tess had met her once. Both were terrified at the sight of the hollow-faced old woman on the tilted hospital bed and overwhelmed by the parade of strange adults who chided them for being strangers.

"We never see you," said Brian's father. "Might as well have moved to Mars."

It had been the same in Syracuse. Clare's family hugged her but with the reserve of resentment. Distant relatives felt the need to tell her and Brian and the children who the dead man was, and what he cared about toward the end of his life. "He cared about family," Aunt Mary said. "He wanted his family close."

Clare worried about the Fourth of July picnic before they left Kodiak. She had already purchased some supplies and wanted to share them, to make sure she could contribute. Jan Lind, three houses down, said, "Jeez, Clare, don't worry about it. We'll have fun." Jan hosted the party, and she was right; we had fun.

Brian called Clyde Carlson from Syracuse to tell him that he couldn't make the Karluk trip and that his mother had had a stroke and that he was sorry to mess up the plan. Brian remembered the four-hour time difference and waited until the afternoon to call. Clyde said not to give it a second thought because John Weddle had originally wanted to come along anyway and that they wouldn't lose the deposit and it would be no problemo. "And," said Clyde, "don't do too much shopping while you guys are down there or Holly is going to bug me about going to Seattle in the fall."

Brian's mother died a week later, and the Bowers felt like outsiders at the funeral. When he was young, Brian had imagined speaking at the funerals of his parents, but no one asked him to do so now. He and Clare and the girls sat as a priest who Brian did not recognize celebrated the life of his mother. During Mass, only Brian took communion. Clare and the girls looked on, estranged.

When the Bowers finally came back, flying from Pittsburgh to Seattle to Anchorage to Kodiak's shack of an airport, their house stood empty and dark. A message from Jan Lind on their answering machine wondered whether Clare had bought plastic cups for the Fourth of July party, because she didn't see them when she checked in their garage. The Bowers went to bed.

Over the following days the weather changed. The rain turned cold. The air went damp and chill, suggesting fall, such as we have it in Kodiak. Black cottonwoods dumped their leaves on our roofs, and we climbed ladders to clear the gutters. Big heart-shaped leaves gone yellow and fetid in the plugged channels.

The Swanson's kid, Mark, looked after the Bower girls' guinea pig while they were gone. He told us that he went over to their house a few days after they got back to return their key and give them the receipts for Cedar's food and bedding, like Brian had told him to. He said the house was dark and that they were all just sitting on the long couch, facing the window, looking across the lawn out onto the street, watching the cars and people pass. Brian had stubble on his face and his clothes were rumpled. He wrote Mark a check for six dollars and forty-three cents. What's a kid supposed to do with a check like that?

"I wonder," mused Dee Carlson to her husband, "whether they're going to do the picnic for the Fourth next year, because Jan said she was going to do it again."

16

The Bowers' house stayed dark. The weather socked in, low clouds with a cold, grim drizzle day after day. They didn't call to ask if anyone could babysit. They didn't host any dinners. We'd see them occasionally around town. Clare and the girls at Kraft's buying groceries. Brian at the post office, collecting their mail. They seemed changed. Their smiles were glassy and stretched. The girls were sullen and pale behind their bangs. They were downcast as they stood in line to buy their canned goods and wilted produce. Someone at the post office asked Brian about the upcoming basketball season, and Brian stared at him blankly. They all seemed to stare at us blankly, the Bowers, as though we had pocketed a gift without saying thank you.

"Sure I feel bad about it," said Clyde Carlson, "but when the reds are running you got to go. It's not like we could have waited."

Then one morning, it was a Tuesday, approaching lunch hour, Brian unlatched the front door of their large white house and led his family single file onto the lawn. Clare held his hand tightly. Emily clutched her mother's hand and pulled Tess behind her. They walked down the three concrete steps, prickly and cold against their bare feet, and stepped onto the grass. There were magpies gathered on their lawn, garish screeching birds that took to the dark spruce trees as the family approached. The Bowers stood there on the lawn, naked, genitals exposed, skin puckering and blue in the chill, faces twisted, beseeching, holding hands. Giving us the gift of their grief, obliging us to receive it.

Old Jacob was there the morning the Bowers stood on their lawn. We saw him standing apart from the crowd across the street when the police came. He watched for a moment and then put his thick hands deep into the pockets of his gray halibut jacket and turned away, walking alone while we all gawked.

17

When the police came, parking in the Bowers' driveway and walking firmly across the lawn, the Bowers appeared resigned, almost meek. Clare was quiet, looking at her feet. The children whimpered as the police grabbed their wrists to pull their hands apart. The police covered their narrow backs with coats and safety blankets. Brian seemed feverish. He spoke to the police.

"Do you see?" Brian asked, slapping his chest, leaving red marks on his skin. "Nothing else matters." He spoke emphatically, backing away as a cop approached. "Nothing but this. This. This is all there is. We came naked; we go naked. Nothing else means anything. You should know. You all should know. Nothing."

"I know," said the cop. His name was Ed Spencer. His daughter Melanie had been a Little Dribbler, attending Brian's basketball camp. "I know," he said. Ed cupped his hand over Brian's head as he eased him into the backseat of the cruiser, protecting him against hitting the edges.

Weeks after, in the rain, there was the Fisherman's Festival down by the harbor. Rides and fair food. Gaunt carnies at the ass-end of the world, sending our townspeople up on a small Ferris wheel and spinning them on slingshot carriages with parts missing. There was the treasure hunt in the parking lot across from the boat harbor, where coins and gumball toys were hidden in a pile of sawdust from the sawmill, and our children dug with abandon into the chips until their pants sagged with damp splinters that made them cry.

Old Jacob Panamarioff sat on a dock rail, drinking from a traveler of vodka in a paper sack, scowling as we passed. Jacob who lived outdoors and smelled of creosote and wool and seaweed. Jacob the creole. Jacob like the desert fathers on Spruce Island, who wept at night on the steps of the Orthodox Church. "All is vanity," says Jacob.

18

"Give me a dollar," says Jacob. "I am the least among you," says Jacob. But now Old Jacob scowled, his burning eyes fixed upon us. Now he said, "You people."

"Christ," said Holly Carlson, "they should do something about him."

We didn't talk much about the Bowers as we moved through the festival. They were leaving Kodiak. Perhaps they had already left. Tina Weddle would teach fourth grade now, as she had wanted to. The district was advertising for a second-grade teacher to fill her position, but we knew it would be fine, even so close to the beginning of school year.

"It's good that it happened during summer," said Jan Lind. When winter things mattered less.

The wind was picking up. A southeast wind, blowing the rain in gusts. It was cold. We were ill from funnel cake and corndogs. We had spent our money. We had thrown dirty softballs at milk bottles and won nothing. The rides had stopped and were being dismantled so the carnies could catch the next ferry off the island. It was time to go home.

Brian and Clare had both pleaded guilty to disorderly conduct and exposure. Their children had been removed by the Division of Family and Youth Services. Their house was for sale. The real estate agent had painted over the large *B*, but the palimpsest was visible if you knew where to look. We all knew where to look.

Soon the fishermen would return and the tourists would leave and the summer would be over. As we walked along the docks, clutching our candy apples and watching the last of the king crab races, we knew fall was upon us and that we could turn our minds toward the business of winter. When it would get dark at three in the afternoon. When we hunkered down. When people stayed inside their houses.

forest

JOE WHITMORE WAS A SEINER OUT OF KODIAK. One summer morning he took his boat out alone and didn't come back. The Coast Guard found the *Glory B* days later, tied up clean at the transient float in Homer. A half mug of coffee sloshed gently on the galley table, atop a signed note that read in its entirety, "Fuck You." He left a wife and two children and a malamute dog in a log house set back in the woods above Mill Bay. No one in Kodiak ever heard from him again.

After the Coast Guard reported the boat found and apparently abandoned, a steady wash of rumor moved through the town. People sorting their mail at the tables in the post office or standing in line at

Kraft's grocery tossed out dark theories: debt, infidelity, elaborate foul play. But few people knew Joe Whitmore well enough to go beyond idle speculation. He wasn't a highliner and had been in the seine fleet for only six or seven years, not long by local standards.

The town knew even less about his wife, Meredith. From the Midwest somewhere, they thought. Some knew her in passing from the daughter being in school, but Meredith avoided parent activities and their guesses about her remained just that. She took a sewing class at the community college when they first moved to town. Someone recalled that she threw a fit when she couldn't get the plaid of a shirt to line up right. Jen Gilpatrick had been there. "A strange woman," she commented later, hiking her eyebrows and shrugging her shoulders as though to indicate there was little more to say. "Sort of stuck up. She seemed unhappy."

After the Coast Guard found the boat and called off the search, the *Glory B*'s three crewmen parked on the road and walked up the trail to the cabin. The cabin sat on a rise in the woods, well back from the bluffs of the bay. The pulling ocean sounded faintly through the shadowed forest of spruce trees. The cabin was built with round logs, chinked with tar. It hadn't been maintained against the wet climate of southwest Alaska. Black moss grew freely on the rotting logs; ditch grass sprouted on the shingles. A thick-billed raven hunched darkly on the roof ridge. It swiveled its attention to the men as they entered the clearing and then spread its wings from its chest and flew off, croaking.

The three crewmen climbed the worn half-log steps up to the listing porch. The skiffman, being older and experienced, led the delegation. The other two weren't more than boys. They found jobs on the *Glory B* by walking the docks two months before and were still green. One was drunk, having discovered nothing better to do while idle ashore.

The malamute dog lay on the threshold of the porch, watching the approach of the three warily. A large square dog, with near black eyes and white paws the size of a man's fist. His thick fur was burred with bits of devil's club and wrinkling green scraps of prickled salmonberry leaf. The drunk boy knelt and stroked the dog's broad muzzle, swaying slightly on his haunches as he did so. The dog's tail thumped once or twice against the porch but his wariness remained.

The skiffman stepped around the dog and knocked firmly on the plankwood door, scuffing the mud from his boots as he waited. The door had no provision for a lock, just a handle and a latch. After a moment the latch sprang and the pale face of a spindly girl peered out from the crack. She wore a blue crocheted poncho and pajama bottoms. She clutched a book of fairy stories to her chest.

"Is your dad home yet?" asked the skiffman.

The girl stared up at him without speaking and then shook her head a quick inch on either side, retreating as Meredith came to the door.

"What do you want?" Meredith asked. She was short, with dirty blonde hair cut in a bowl shape that framed her round face. She wore a bulky brown-and-white Icelandic sweater over a pair of jeans. She looked at the skiffman with red eyes, her expression slack and unfriendly.

"Came for our checks," said the skiffman. "We fished half the season and are due to get paid."

When she did not respond, he continued. "I've got copies of the fish tickets and Joe's agreement on our crewshares right here if you want to see." He dug beneath his orange raincoat and came out with a soiled manila envelope, scratched over with Joe's handwriting.

Meredith regarded the three men sourly, her eyes lingering for a moment on the drunk one. He was bent awkwardly at the waist with one hand in his jeans pocket and the other fumbling for a cigarette rolling away from him on the porch. She ignored the envelope.

"He owes you. I don't," she said.

"We don't know where he is," said the skiffman.

"Me neither."

The skiffman exhaled and ran his tongue over his lower teeth. A grubby boy came up behind Meredith, circling her around the leg with one arm, leaving the other hand free to pull on a piece of string he was chewing. The dingy toe-ends of his socks flapped as he shifted his small weight, eyeing the men.

"Noah, go and play with Grace," she said sharply, brushing him back. The boy slunk out of sight into the dim stillness of the cabin.

"Look, Mrs. Whitmore," said the skiffman when the boy was gone, "we're owed a fair pot of money, and we don't want to have to sue you for it." The drunk nodded loosely behind him. The third crewman leaned against the porch rail, arms crossed.

Meredith snorted and turned down the corners of her mouth as if she had tasted something foul, her face contorting. "Sue him," she spat.

The skiffman flinched back as though struck. He still held the soiled envelope in his hand. He folded it along a worn crease and tucked it back into the belly pocket of his sweatshirt.

"Whatever," he said finally, turning to leave. "We'll be in touch."

As the three men stomped down off the porch, Meredith stepped halfway out of the door. "If you find that sonofabitch," she yelled, "tell him to come get his fucking dog." She slammed the door. The sound echoed through the woods like a rifle shot.

Meredith leaned against the rough planking of the closed door for a moment and then walked to the kitchen table. She sat heavily, the legs of the chair scraping. Her breath convulsed, shuddering her body, and she wept. Grace stood at the picture window next to the stonework fireplace, watching the men leave the clearing and disappear into the trees as they followed the trail back to the road. Her eyes tracked the safety orange of the skiffman's slicker, winking brightly through the thicket of goat's beard and baneberry that encroached upon the clearing, until he disappeared in the darkness of the wood. Noah, with his flapping socks, stood mute between them in the heavy air of the cabin, chewing the string until the strands split against the roof of his mouth.

Meredith sat at the table all afternoon, staring blankly at the visible grain of its polished wood. Occasionally she'd remove a fraying wad of tissue from the sleeve of her sweater and wipe her nose, rocking softly against the back of the chair.

The children put themselves to bed early, Grace nudging Noah along. They slept in the same room, small beds on either side of a window that opened to the back of the cabin, facing the inevitable junkyard of a commercial fisherman: piles of rotting seine web, engine parts, stacks of crab pots, coils of line, discarded kickers rusting half hidden in the tall fireweed.

When the children were quiet, Meredith stood and filled a glass of water from the kitchen tap. It was well water, pungent and rust colored. She drank it down and filled it again, drinking the second glass quickly, eyes fixed and blank, her breath gulping and labored from the effort. She set the glass on the counter and walked to the door. The latch stuck slightly, from having been slammed.

On the porch she pulled on her boots. She did not look at the dog, who curled his head toward her with benign interest. She stomped her feet into the boots as she strode to the back of the porch, where it was level with the ground, and began picking through the junk behind the cabin.

She found a section of rebar that Joe had bent into a right angle to reinforce the corner of a crab pot and a yellow coil of stiffly braided nylon line. She carried them both to an open patch of ground between the trees just beyond the clearing. She pushed the ends of the rebar into the soil as far as she could and then walked around to the wood-pile in front of the cabin, returning to the open patch with the ax dragging behind her.

She pounded the rebar into the ground with the butt of the ax head, holding it tight like a hammer at first and then swinging it full, the wood of the handle neck splintering against the steel bar when she missed.

With the rebar stuck firmly in the ground, only a shallow triangle showing above the dirt, she fixed one end of the rope to it with a lopsided series of square knots. She tugged against it to test, leaning back with her weight. Then she dropped the rope end and walked back to the porch.

The dog was sleeping at the threshold of the door and blinked at Meredith groggily when she stood over him.

"Get up," she said.

The dog raised his head, but did not otherwise stir. Meredith gripped the dog by the fur of his neck and pulled him sharply upright. The dog stood, confused, and shook himself. She lost her grip when he shook, so she took him again and pulled him along the porch to the open space. The dog balked at first, nails scratching on the porch, and then trotted alongside willingly as though invited to a game.

She took the free rope end and tied a collar around the dog's neck, tying the same series of square knots as on the rebar. Then she turned back to the house. The dog started to follow but heaved up short when the line went taut. The dog watched her intently, ears forward, as she stepped up onto the porch and reentered the cabin.

Meredith came back onto the porch with a half-full bag of dog food hoisted on her shoulder, the sack paper crinkling in her ear. She carried it down the log steps and set off on the trail to the road. It was well into evening, near eleven o'clock, but the sky was still light and she knew the path well enough that even amidst the gloom of the trees she did not stumble. The path led around red gnarls of tree root and was bordered for a stretch with white clam shells and sea glass collected and arranged by Grace the year before.

She came out of the trees and stepped up the loose grade to the gravel road. Joe's blue pickup sat parked on a potholed apron near the trail. Meredith dumped the bag of dog food into the back of the truck. It landed heavily, spilling brown marbles of kibble loose into the wet wales of the truck bed. She wiped her hands on her jeans and turned back to the cabin. Through the trees she could hear the dog already barking.

Meredith slept that night in her clothes, after first pulling shut the heavy drapes against the uncanny blue twilight that lingered until dawn. Noah's hand pushing on her shoulder roused her awake. He stood next to the bed in his pajamas, working a bent thumb into his nose absentmindedly.

"It's morning," he said. "How come Jonas is tied up?"

Meredith blinked at him, as though he were a stranger. There were red welts on her face where she had slept on her sweater, twisting in the night. The boy breathed loudly through his mouth as he continued working the thumb.

"He's sick," she said. "Don't go near him."

"But he's barking a lot."

"Because he's sick. You and Grace just leave him alone, okay?"

Noah nodded slowly, breathing.

"Please stop picking your nose."

He removed his thumb and examined it briefly. "How come you're wearing all your clothes?"

"Because I'm feeling sick, too. Both of you just need to leave me alone."

Meredith rolled away and pulled the blanket to her face. Noah stood for a few minutes, shifting his weight from foot to foot, tentative and uncertain, and then shuffled out of the dark room, closing the door behind him.

For the next two days Meredith rarely left her bed. The dog barked and howled without cease. The children watched the dog from the edge of the clearing, not daring to approach. The dog lunged wildly against the rope, running like a compass-pencil at the extent of the tether, inscribing a bitter circle in the earth. At times the dog would drop, panting, into a crouch. The rope was burning away the thick fur of the dog's neck, exposing a rust-colored ring of scored flesh.

"Do you wanna go throw rocks?" asked Noah.

Grace shook her head slowly, not looking at him, transfixed by the dog.

Noah shrugged and wandered away slack jawed, picking his nose. He gathered a pocketful of gravel and squatted next to the well, some thirty paces from the front of the cabin, down a gentle slope. The well was four-foot square at the surface, a deep hole with heavy black visqueen sheathing the sides. A short timber frame anchored the plastic and supported the scrap plywood cover. Noah shoved a corner of the cover back and shivered at the dank cold air that escaped.

The water was two feet below the opening, dark and scummed with spruce needles. Noah dropped his collection of stones into the well one at a time, listening intently to each splash, like a catch of breath, as they fell.

When he ran out of rocks, Noah found a toy that his father had given him, forgotten in the growing weeds under the porch. A heavy Kong ape figure, rubbery and filled with gel that allowed its limbs to stretch when pulled. Noah took the doll to the woodpile and dismembered it on the chopping block, striking it intently with the hatchet. The red gel oozed forth onto the block and smeared the hatchet's pitted blade. Noah gathered up the pieces and threw them into the well, committing them to the water.

On the third or fourth day of steady barking, Pete Dombrowski, a neighbor to the north through the woods, knocked on the door. He and his wife had been guests once or twice at dinner. He'd played cribbage with Joe over coffee and brandy, and had figured what was coming. He wasn't surprised when it did. But he didn't gossip and had kept his mouth shut at the post office while others speculated.

Meredith opened the door and greeted him with a mumble.

"Just checking in, hey," said Pete, tall and grinning, holding out a package the size of a bread loaf wrapped in brown butcher paper. "Some halibut for you guys. Caught it yesterday. It'll freeze just like this if you've no call for it in the next few days."

Meredith made no move to take it. "We're okay," she said.

"Oh, sure you are," said Pete. "We just had some extra. Caught it on sport gear, hey. Can't sell it." He thrust the package toward her and she took it reluctantly.

"So you're fine?"

"We're fine."

"Good, hey." Pete smiled and nodded. "Give me or Rose a call if you need anything. Anything at all."

Meredith nodded and closed the door. Pete stood for a moment and then walked to the back edge of the porch, rubbing his hands together, chilled from carrying the halibut. His face flattened as he watched the dog, crouched in the dirt, panting heavily. Pete spit and walked home through the trees.

Meredith dropped the package on the kitchen table and sat with her hands clutched white in her lap, staring into the middle distance. Grace approached carefully, placing her fingertips on the edge of the table as though addressing a piano.

"Why can't we feed Jonas?" she asked.

"If your father wants to feed him, he can."

"But . . ."

Meredith slapped her palm flat on the table hard. Grace jumped back, hiding her fingers in protective fists. The noise burst in the kitchen and then faded, ringing in the air. Meredith stared down at the table and spoke evenly, with a high edge to her voice, emphasizing every word. "I am doing the best that I can," she said. "I'm doing the best I can." She sniffled and pulled the gray wad of tissue from her sleeve. Grace stepped away, unnoticed, not turning her back until she had reached the living room.

That afternoon the electric pump in the well quit and they had to carry water buckets for washing and flushing the toilet. Meredith lost her temper at the sputtering faucets, slamming the cabinets and stomping on her heels as she walked, fuming. Noah grew sullen, fretting guiltily around the mouth of the well, staring into black depths.

While the children hauled the splashing buckets of brown water up from the well, Meredith calmed and seemed to rally. She busied herself in the kitchen, cooking some of the halibut and baking a batch of oatmeal cookies, which Grace especially admired. They sat at the table with only three chairs. Meredith lit a candle stub to place between them and hummed while she served the dinner. The children ate quietly, forks tapping against the plates. Meredith smiled broadly at them both and proposed a toast to adventure. "Everything new begins from now on," she said. The hoarse voice of the dog continued to sound outside.

Noah ate steadily, but Grace only picked at her food. When Meredith went to the bathroom, Grace's plate was still full. Grace waited until the bathroom door closed and then she stood, holding her plate before her carefully, and went outside. Noah watched her unlatch the door and step onto the porch.

"Mom," he called. "Mom! Grace is feeding Jonas."

Meredith ran from the bathroom, jeans unzipped, and stormed onto the porch. Noah heard yelling, and the sound the of the plate breaking. Meredith swept back into the house wrenching Grace by the arm, dragging her to the bedroom. The door slammed. The silverware on the table jumped. There were muffled cries.

Noah sat alone at the table, swinging his legs and eating through the stack of cookies. He chewed, letting the crumbs flake onto his lap, as the candle guttered down into its socket, casting lurching shadows against the walls.

They awoke the next morning to silence and found the dog gone. The rust-colored collar of rope lay empty in the dirt, pulled free in the night. Over the next few days, the children would occasionally see the dog coursing through the forest, skinny and wild. Grace called when she saw him, but the dog did not turn or slow. He howled in the night, demoralized and haunted. Neighbors found their rabbit hutches tipped and their yards torn with blood and fur. Someone came across a deer mauled in the thicket. A Labrador was killed.

Meredith took a job at the cannery, working long hours on the slime line and picking shrimp with taciturn Filipino women for overtime. When she came home to fall into exhausted sleep, the children would retch at the gutty stench of her clothes.

Grace was left in charge of Noah during the day, but she refused to speak with him. Only once did she acknowledge him at all.

"Do you wanna throw rocks?" he asked.

Grace looked at him square. "You bastard," she said.

He shuffled away, thumb working in his nose, and neither spoke further.

One afternoon, Grace sat idle on the chopping block, reading her book of stories and picking at splinters when she saw Pete Dombrowski step into the clearing. He walked slowly and had a black-barreled deer rifle slung on a leather strap on his shoulder. Grace regarded him with alarm. She stood barefoot in the scattered wood chips.

"What are you doing?" she asked.

"Nothing, sweetheart," said Pete, shaking his head. "Just going for a walk."

"I know . . ." said Grace. "I know what you are doing."

Pete stopped and looked at her and nodded once. "Then you should go inside."

Grace clutched at her patchwork skirt and stared at Pete intently. "We're not okay," she said with rising panic in her voice. "We're not okay."

Pete swallowed and pressed his lips together. "I know, kiddo," he said. "I know that." He stared at her for a moment longer and then turned and stalked slowly out of the clearing, threading his way noiselessly through the trees.

An hour or so later a shot rang out sharply in the distance, then another, then silence. Noah was squatting at the lip of the well. He stood at the noise and looked toward Grace, standing on the porch. He saw her face go white and then crumple red before she turned and went inside.

Noah squatted again. Floating below on the surface of the well were the remnants of the Kong doll. The heavy gel had dissolved, leaving the cut pieces of rubber to rise to the surface. Noah fished at them with a length of spruce branch, hooking one, a leg, which he buried in a roothole. He swiped at the others as they bobbed out of reach, sinking under. He leaned, stretching forward over the dark water with the stick, bracing his leg against the wooden lip of the well. A rotted section gave way; the board slapped flat against the ground as it pulled from the nails. Noah pitched, thrashing into the water, gripping the spruce branch tightly in his fist. The branch stiffened against the wall as he fell, and the jagged end in his hand pushed sharply into his face. He felt a searing pain and tried to scream but he was beneath the water. He thrashed and scrabbled until his head was clear, and then he screamed and screamed.

That night, after the hospital, after the yelling and the crying, when the cabin was dark and silent, Noah lay in his bed feverish and in pain. A huge gauze patch was taped over his left eye, and orange iodine smears covered the scratches on his face and arms. Grace lay awake in her bed nearby, listening to his ragged and whimpering breath. She set aside her book of stories and slid from beneath the blankets. She crawled next to him, wrapping her spindly arms around him firmly and gently, rocking him in the dark.

"Shh," she said, "shhh."

"Oh god," said Noah, gulping. "It hurts it hurts it hurts."

"Hush now," soothed Grace, petting him.

Noah shook and whimpered in her arms. She whispered in his ear. "You must be strong. You are a pirate now. You will wear a patch and sail the pirate seas. You are like Odin now. Hush."

Outside the wind rose in the night, creaking the darkening wood that grew ever closer upon the cabin. The children held each other, centered in the darkness at the edge of the world. The wind howled. A haunted sound, moaning through the trees.

*what this guy
said one
night, in the
arctic bar,
in juneau,
alaska*

MY GRANDDAD THOUGHT ALL HIS SONS WERE IDIOTS, so on his death-
bed he refused to tell them anything. He said he had a revelation
about how to live a good life and be rich and happy, but that none
of his children were worthy of hearing such wisdom. My daddy was
one of those sons, and I agree. They were all a bunch of fuckups.

Even with shit-brain sons, my granddad didn't want his hard-won
revelation to go to waste. Instead of speaking it aloud, where anyone
could hear, he whispered whatever he'd learned or understood or seen
or realized into an empty whiskey bottle and corked his words firmly

inside. Our family's heritage, invisible within the brown glass of a traveler of Ten High.

When I was sixteen, and living in his basement, I asked my uncle Bill about it. He said that Granddad was a cussed asshole and the only thing he ever put in an empty bottle was spit. But my uncle saved the wisdom bottle all the same and kept it on a utility shelf next to a softball-league trophy. One night in a rage I ripped the felt on my uncle's pool table and pulled the utility shelf down with a crash. The bottle broke and the glass scattered and my uncle descended the steps from the kitchen above, stark naked. He eyeballed first the wreckage, and then me. He didn't say anything and I didn't either. And I know in that silence we were both listening for my granddad's words. I didn't hear anything, and I don't think Uncle Bill did. I figured, though, that I'd better leave.

The wind blew west that night, and I followed it. I wouldn't have said it then, because it seemed silly, but I suppose I thought the words would catch up in that wind, so it was the right direction to go. I walked and hitchhiked and hustled, trying to get ahead of it, but I never could. Through Kansas and Oklahoma, California, Oregon. I kept my ears peeled.

On my travels I heard many strange things. I heard of this old woman who raised her eyebrows so hard in surprise that she rose a foot into the air and almost flew. I heard of a man who cut out his own tongue with a chisel to make a point. And a basenji dog that could pick winning Powerball numbers by scent. People said that the woman was a witch, and the man was a fool, and the dog was a saint. I don't know if any of it is true. I wasn't listening for it. Just things people said.

I'm fifty now and still haven't heard my granddad's words. I know they're out there. Blowing around some ice field up in the mountains.

The Chilkats, maybe. I listen to the Taku winds when they come, standing out in the cold all night sometimes. How would you find such a thing? One white whale in all these oceans? But I won't quit. When I've heard what every empty whisky bottle in here has to say, I'll move on. Up to Haines, probably. I tell you though, people break my heart. Every single one of them does.

blue ticket

IT WAS EARLY OCTOBER AND RAINING AND NEAR DARK when Amos arrived at the squatter's camp. Russell watched him come up the trail and stop, uncertain. Amos looked boyish, eighteen at most. Scrawny and hollow faced. It appeared that he'd cut his own hair, hacked his own thin beard, with a knife. The only thing he carried was a scrap of visqueen that he rolled about himself to keep the rain off while he slept, tucked into the one-walled crease of a roofless mining bunker.

The squatter's camp was a mile south of Juneau, hidden in the woods two hundred feet back above Thane Road. Fifteen or so sagging tents and various lean-tos made from blue tarps and warping plywood.

The forest was littered with the remnants of the Alaska-Juneau Mine: concrete ruins and rusting hulks of inexplicable machinery. The squatters lived among the ruins and between the spruce trees, adding their wreckage to the decaying past: soggy mattresses and drifts of beer cans. Some people stayed for a week, others longer. Russell had been there since June and was scared he would die there alone and unacknowledged.

The next morning, Russell pushed out of his sleeping bag and unzipped the door of his tent. Amos sat on a log next to a dead fire, wet and shivering, hands between his legs as though in hidden prayer. Russell regarded him for a moment before speaking. The boy's clothes were ragged. A pair of duck-cloth pants, a homemade plaid shirt with carefully matched seams, a thin parka. All soaked through. He looked worse off than Russell did when Fat George took him under his wing. With Fat George gone, Russell felt the obligation to help the boy.

"Hey," Russell said. "Get any sleep?"

Amos dipped his head in a nodding shrug, seeming to fold farther into his frame. Russell waited for him to raise his head and meet his eyes, but he didn't. Russell coughed wetly and leaned out of the tent to spit. He set his stiff leather boots outside the tent and stepped into them as he emerged. "Give me a second," he said. He shuffled to a patch of devil's club and pissed and then walked back to where Amos sat by the dead fire, pausing to turn his torso sharply, cracking his spine.

"What's your name?" asked Russell.

"Amos."

"I'm Russell. I bet you didn't sleep at all."

"I've slept worse," said Amos. His voice was a strange mumble. It sounded somehow antique.

"I'll make a fire," said Russell. He'd never built a fire before getting stuck in Juneau, but now he prided himself on his skill at nursing wood into combustion. When the fire held, he squatted across the fire pit from Amos and fed larger, wetter branches that popped and hissed in the dawn. The heavy smoke stung his eyes, but the fire was warm. He watched Amos unfold and ease in the heat, straightening his back and letting his legs splay open. Steam rose from the cuffs of his pants. Russell fed another branch into the fire and sat back on a log. It satisfied him to see the boy warming. He felt an impulse to make coffee or hot chocolate or oatmeal. Something to offer. For the last week he had been finishing a tub of peanut butter, scooping it out with his fingers in a way that would be depressing to an observer. The grooves of his fingers against the greased plastic jar were depressing even to him. It could not be shared. But in the hierarchy of human need, when it's raining, food comes second. So Russell considered that.

"That tent over there is empty," said Russell, pointing. "You can sleep in it until you figure something else out."

Amos stared at the tent, a lime-green A-frame style with a single ridgepole across the top, sides sagging. "Whose is it?"

Russell could hear the camp stirring. The usual coughs and groans.

"It belongs to a guy named George. Fat George."

"Where's he at?"

"Lemon Creek." Amos's face remained blank, leaving the question in the air. "Jail," Russell added.

Amos stared at the tent again, seeming to weigh the option. "For what?" he asked.

Russell shrugged. "A cop tapped him on the shoulder while he was pissing in the doorway of a restaurant downtown. George was so drunk he turned around and splashed the cop's shoes. He'll be out in a week or so." Russell added another branch to the fire. "George won't mind. He likes to help people out. You warm now?"

Amos nodded.

"Then get some sleep." Russell checked his watch. "It's not even eight yet."

After Amos disappeared into the tent, Russell stared at the fire a while longer. He felt the pinch of his stomach but the idea of the peanut butter made him ill. He had forty dollars left. As he listened to the camp waken, as puffy-eyed men straggled to the fire and sat heavily, he decided to walk to town and spend some of it. Make a meal he could share.

Russell's remaining forty dollars represented a heroic act of financial management. He had five hundred dollars when he came to Juneau in the spring. He'd gone to Alaska to escape Seattle. To get away from Second and Pike. He hitchhiked to Bellingham and took the ferry north to start over and make money and get clean. At thirty-two, a fresh start still felt possible. He rented a week-rate room at the Alaskan Hotel and looked for a job. Everyone said he'd come at the wrong time. Summer jobs were booked. Maybe try back later, after the seasonal turnover. Maybe in the fall. After that first week Russell had two hundred thirty-two dollars and a tent and a sleeping bag. Another week's rent would clear him out, so he turned back his key. He camped the first night in Cope Park where a mustached cop moved him along before dawn. He shivered in the bus shelter downtown for hours until he met Fat George, who wandered south toward Thane in the evening and told Russell to follow. After four months, Russell felt much older.

Here's how Russell aged: Early on, in June, he visited the library every morning and perused the paper. He scanned the sparse want ads in the *Juneau Empire* and followed the news. Occasionally he would leaf through a GED study guide and jot answers on a piece of scrap paper with a stubby pencil from the tray by the card catalog. In the afternoon he would spring four dollars for a bagel and a cup of brewed coffee from Heritage and stroll along the cruise ship docks, feeling faintly superior to the tourists. He was young and local and regenerating and clean. The squawking rain-ponchoed hoards were just visiting. In the evening he ambled back toward camp. He had a rod and reel and angled off the beach below Thane Road, catching a Dolly Varden or humpy for dinner. It was not bad. Almost civilized. He could conserve cash and wait until fall. But the want ads stayed sparse, and the dirt took its toll. By August the tourists looked away from him with studiously blank expressions. Homeless is homeless no matter where. He skipped the library and ate the free bum lunch at the Treadwell Kitchen on South Franklin. Some nights he loitered at the Imperial Bar, drinking water or cheap burnt coffee. Waiting for a happy drunk to win big on rippies and ring the bell. A round for everyone. Then he'd walk home. By September, Russell's cheeks had sunk and his beard had grown and he left the camp only if he had to.

The camp changed through the summer, too. For a month of good weather it was like a drunken carnival swap meet. There were late nights and bonfires. The northern lights curtained the sky above the mountains. People came and went and shared suitcases of Rainier and convenience-store cold cuts. Their laughter echoed off the mining ruins and their humping shadows splayed on tent walls. Then came September and the raucous parties died in the rain. Some kids, semi-pro hippies, would show up for a day or two and change their minds. A panicked phone call and a Western Union later they'd tack back to the land of plenty, leaving nothing behind them but the scent of patchouli. Their odor was replaced by old men who stank of mouth-wash and aftershave and perfume. Fat George, with a traveler of whiskey, roaring and shaking his hairless belly in the firelight. Russell had a phone number and had called it twice in his adult life. Once it paid for rehab and the second time it said no. He didn't want to call it again.

It was an hour walk to Foodland from the camp. Down the muddy trail gnarled with spruce roots and hedged by devil's club. North on Thane Road until it turned into South Franklin Street at the edge of town. A dispiriting strip of shuttered tourist shops inter-mixed with bars. The Great Alaskan Tee Shirt Shop, The Rendezvous, Columbian Emeralds, The Lucky Lady, Northland Fur Company, The Arctic Bar. At the corner of Franklin and Front, Russell passed the enclosed city bus shelter where he'd met Fat George. Some people called it the Crystal Palace. Later in the day and through the night it would be full of people from the squatter's camp and other like-minded hobbyists. Drinking from paper bags and marking time by the arrival and departure of busses none of them rode.

Russell crossed Franklin and walked down Main Street, past the Triangle Club and the Imperial Bar. Already a short line of old men fidgeted outside the door of the Triangle, waiting for it to open. Russell walked the rest of the way watching his feet.

When he reached the Foodland parking lot Russell saw two police cars with their disco-lights rolling near the entry. A man he knew from the camp slumped unsteadily on a concrete parking bumper with his legs outstretched and his hands cuffed behind his back. Jerry's pants and the lower half of his white T-shirt were dark with what appeared to be blood. Russell stopped short. Two cops stood nearby with a woman dressed to the store's code, a maroon vest and a name badge. A stack of plastic-wrapped meat and two disposable cameras tottered on the hood of one of the cop cars.

"Hey Russell," Jerry drawled, grinning, as though his situation was a fine joke. "Thought they shot me but it was just the steaks in my pants broke open." One of the cops turned and stared hard at Russell. Jerry kept talking. "Keep an eye on my shit will you?"

"Move on," said the cop. Russell nodded and went into the store. He spent nineteen dollars on coffee, three cans of condensed soup, two boxes of tuna helper, oatmeal, and a box of powdered milk. He decided against the hot chocolate and the new toothbrush. A young Filipino girl took his money without looking at him.

It was drizzling when Russell made it back to camp. The fire smoldered but there was no one about. Russell stowed the groceries and then stood next to the lime-green tent, listening for Amos's breathing. He heard the boy stir. "You awake?"

"Sort of," said Amos.

"Sleep more if you need to," said Russell. "I'm going fishing. Catch something for lunch. Come if you want." Russell gathered his gear and was heading toward the trail when Amos unzipped his tent. Russell waited for him to catch up and then proceeded. Thane Road runs along the shore of Gastineau Channel, a cold, deep finger of the Pacific that cuts between the mainland and Douglas Island. Russell and Amos crossed the road and stepped down the steep embankment onto the rocky beach, grabbing at branches of scrub willow and alder to steady their descent.

The tideline of the beach was littered with scoured logs and driftwood and marine trash: chunks of cork from seine floats, sun-bleached and deflated buoys, milk jugs, useless lengths of fraying rope. Russell led the way down the beach toward the stubby point where he liked to fish. Amos followed, walking carefully on the slick barnacled rocks, his arms outstretched for balance.

At the point, Russell geared up his rod. It was a short button caster, the kind generally used by children just learning to fish. Russell found it at Sally Ann's for three dollars—a package deal with four pixie spoons. He set his feet and cast awkwardly. The drizzle continued from the low mat of gray cloud, but there was no wind to stir the slack ocean. The spoon arced out in the air silently, like a raised eyebrow, hitting the water with a fleeting gulp. Russell reeled back quickly and cast again.

"This has been an okay spot for me," he said. "I caught a lot of humpies in the summer. Dolly Varden too." He cast easily now. Another fleeting gulp. "We'll catch something. Even if we don't, I got some other groceries."

Amos stood a few paces behind and to the left of Russell to be out of the way of the hook on the backswing. He held a mussel shell in his hand, rubbing his thumb in its smooth pearled chamber. "Thank you," he said. Russell shrugged his shoulders slightly.

"I mean it," said Amos. "I thank you for your kindness. I didn't know what I was going to do."

Russell looked back at him over his shoulder. "It's nothing," he said, casting again. Gulp. "Where are you from?"

"Skagway. North of Skagway."

"Take the ferry down?"

"No. I walked."

Russell turned back and looked at him. "You walked?" Amos nodded. "Jesus," said Russell loudly. Amos's face flinched, a momentary squint and twist of his cheeks, as though something had been thrown at him. Russell took a moment to reel in the line.

"You walked with no tent? Nothing?"

Amos looked down, focusing on the nacreous shine of the mussel shell. "I had things," he answered simply. "I just lost them is all. I had to swim once and I lost them in the water."

Russell shook his head, marveling. "Well that is something else, my friend. You're lucky to be alive."

Amos gave a fleeting half smile, an abbreviated twisting grin. "I was scared," he said. "I shouldn't say so, but I'd be lying if I said I wasn't."

"Everybody's scared of something," said Russell. "It's okay to say so."

They fished a while longer, following the lapping edge of the water as the tide ebbed slowly down the beach, uncovering rust-orange rockweed and wet pockets of squirming blennies. Things trapped and left behind by the sea. Russell caught two small Dollies in quick succession. He gutted them out on a flat rock, leaving the ropy entrails for the ravens eyeing him from the branches of a nearby cottonwood. Amos gathered an armload of driftwood for the fire and they headed back to camp, struggling up the muddy trail, breathing hard.

Amos built a fire on the coals left from the morning while Russell wrapped the fish in a creased scrap of tinfoil and read the instructions on a box of tuna helper. With the fire going, Amos sat back and began to whittle on a long thin piece of flat driftwood with a pocketknife. Russell put a rack on the edge of the fire and set the fish upon it, together with a pan of water for boiling.

"So what are you scared of?" asked Amos.

Russell snorted. "Bears. Everything."

"Bears come around much?"

"Once or twice this summer. People get sloppy with their food. I do too sometimes. But we make enough noise, I guess." Russell pushed the fish around on the rack with a stick. His voice grew serious. "I'm scared of being stuck here forever. I've got to start looking for a job again. Can't even afford to leave Juneau right now. Stupid to come to a town with no roads." Then he snorted again. "And I'm not crazy enough to try to walk out of here."

Amos grinned sheepishly. "I wouldn't recommend it to you."

Russell gave Amos his plate and heaped it high when the food was done. He ate his own portion directly from the pan after it cooled. They stared into the fire as they ate. Midway through their meal one of the squatters returned up the trail. A taciturn man named Hugo who never said much but sometimes shouted out in his sleep. Russell offered him a bite, but Hugo shook his head and disappeared behind the flap of his lean-to. Amos scraped his plate clean and belched softly. "It's not so bad when your belly's full, being stuck here. There's worse places."

Russell nodded. He thought of Second and Pike, of waking up sick after lost time, not knowing where he was. "Sure," he said. "I suppose there is."

They remained in camp all day, staring into the fire, talking off and on until nightfall. Russell yawned and dozed and awoke with a start. Amos kept shaping his piece of driftwood until he seemed pleased with it. It was oblong, with notched edges and a dull point, shaped like a spearhead. He carved a hole in one end and asked Russell if he had any twine. Russell nodded and yawned and stood. He shuffled to his tent, feeling the air bite cold away from the fire. He found a tangle of bristling brown twine, the same twine that held up his too-large jeans. He stood over Amos as he watched him fix a length of it to the wood and then begin to twist it.

"What've you got there?" asked Russell.

"It's a wolf roarer," he said. "To keep the bears at bay."

"What, you hit 'em with it?"

Amos looked up with his half smile. "No. It makes a noise. We used to have sheep and goats at our place, and my brothers and I would make these to keep the wolves off. Listen." Amos stood and swung the piece of wood around his head like a lasso, letting out twine so it swung in a widening circle. The wooden piece spun on its axis as the twist in the twine released. The sound it made, doppling as Amos swung faster and wider, was like a slow chain saw, growling and screaming in the dark. There were some half-hearted protests from the men in their grim tents, but Amos kept swinging the wolf roarer, his face lit with firelight. For Russell, the noise was comforting. It gave fear a sound and made it a warning to the surrounding darkness. It echoed in his head as he slept.

In the days that followed, Russell and Amos fell into an easy pattern together: fire and coffee in the morning, fish if they were lucky, or lunch at the Treadwell. Part of each day was dedicated to getting out of the rain. Damp amplified the cold, and they were always damp. Their clothes stank of mildew and wood smoke. Sometimes they spent time in the atrium of the State Office Building. With its skylights and potted trees, the SOB was like a vacation. In the center of the atrium stood a totem pole that Fat George claimed came from his family, but the plaque made no mention of it.

One cold night they went to the Imperial Bar and sipped water while it was still empty enough for the bartender not to care. Russell kept an ear open for someone ringing the bell, but no one had any luck with the rippies. Amos sat uncomfortably, eyes down. He didn't say much, or talk about his past. Russell had gathered that he came from a large religious family that homesteaded land and kept to themselves. His father was dead, and Amos had left for reasons he didn't say. Russell didn't press.

At the other end of the bar, playing pool and feeding the jukebox, clustered a group of loud young men with close-cropped hair and braided belts and gym arms. They laughed and pushed each other and called each other faggots. Russell recognized them as a type and avoided looking their way. When he went to the bathroom though, one of the men was standing at the sink, a small black kit bag open on the counter, a syringe in his hand. Russell froze. He felt his heart lurch and a small sigh escaped him. The man, tall and bulging, with tiny cauliflower ears on either side of a head that itself seemed well-muscled, glowered at him. "What?"

Russell stammered. "Nothing, man. It's just that you shouldn't, you know. I used to—"

"I'm a diabetic, asshole," spat the man. "You homeless hippie faggots make me sick. Get the fuck out of here." Russell's face burned as he left. Amos followed and didn't ask what happened. Russell appreciated that. Sometimes you just left a place quickly for reasons you didn't have to say.

Another week passed before Fat George returned, and when he did it was a big to-do. He embraced everyone, hooting as he pressed them to his stomach. He embraced Amos and thanked him for watching his tent. They made a bonfire and someone supplied hotdogs that they ate right off the sticks with Tabasco sauce. Fat George, fully rested and enjoying a fifth of Country Club, stood on a log and performed his story of pissing on Officer Vandiver's shoes with great animation. "He said to me: 'In the olden days, we'd blue ticket your ass for what you did to my shoes, kick you out of town.' And I said to him: 'You can't blue ticket me, motherfucker, I am Wooshkeetaan, Wolf Eagle, I blue ticket *you*, motherfucker!'" The assembled cheered and Fat George took off his shirt and danced slow and Tlingit in the firelight, singing a song to himself, eyes closed.

It was late when everyone crawled off to sleep, and Russell saw Amos looking uncomfortable, sitting by the dying fire. "Sleep in my tent," said Russell. "There's room. We'll find something else tomorrow." Amos nodded, relief on his face.

When they finished arranging themselves in Russell's small tent, tucked in their sleeping bags and blankets, they were comfortable as could be expected. The camp went quiet but for the creak of the surrounding spruce trees and the occasional ember popping in the fire. Russell felt his breath lengthening, becoming even and heavy as he eased into sleep. It was his favorite time, feeling his body go slack and the heaviness come and his chattering mind go silent.

"Russell?" Amos whispered. "You awake?"

"Huh."

"You awake?"

"Yeah."

The boy was silent for a moment. Then he whispered again. "I was thinking, maybe tomorrow you could cut my hair right. Or we could find someone to cut my hair right. Those people in the bar were looking at me like I was crazy."

"Your hair's a bit uneven," said Russell. "You could wear a hat."

"It used to be long. My beard, too. But it was wispy. My papa said my beard would go full after I had seventeen years but it didn't. He was wrong about that. I cut my hair off with my knife after I left home. I was eager to be rid of it, but I wasn't thinking what it would look like."

Amos's voice came low and ragged. He was on his back, face directed up to the roof of the tent. "I used to think God lived in Papa's beard. When I was a boy. His beard was so long and white and sometimes when the light hit it right it looked like it was on fire. His beard moved and danced when he spoke, and all he spoke was God's word."

Amos took a deep breath. "Or he said it was. I suspect he was wrong about some of that, too."

There was a long silence. Russell felt he should say something. "He passed on, didn't he? Your dad?" Russell heard Amos's nodding head scrape against the sleeping bag.

"He's dead enough," said Amos. There was another long silence, but Russell did not break it. In a moment, Amos spoke again, as though he was picking up from where he left off. "Before I left I took a map that Papa had on the wall in the room where he kept books and other forbidden things. It was a big map, some three foot square. It had never been folded before I folded it. It showed the coast between here and Skagway. I thought I needed it but I didn't. All you do is follow the coast. I didn't need a map for that. Nobody does."

"What do you mean forbidden? You couldn't read books?"

"No," said Amos. "We weren't to read or write. Just to listen when Papa spoke out of his beard."

Russell turned and propped himself up on his elbow, looking at the shape of Amos's face in the darkness. "So you can't read?"

"I can read some. Mother taught us some, on the side."

"So you've never been to a library?" Amos didn't answer.

"Well," said Russell, "that's just crazy. Tomorrow we'll go to the library. It's a good one. We'll go in the afternoon." Russell dropped back flat onto his sleeping bag. "No books allowed," he said, mulling it over. "I can't imagine it. It sounds like leaving was the right thing. Jesus."

"Came here to be punished and ought to be punished," he whispered.

"What?"

"It wasn't just the books that made me leave." Amos's voice was choked, thickening. "I've done bad things, Russell." He heaved a sigh that broke into a jagged sob, the crying of a child, face wet with snot.

He rolled on his side and brought his knees to his chest, curling into a tight ball.

Russell let him cry for a time and then reached his hand over and rubbed his back, soothing him. "It's okay, Amos. We've all done bad things."

The next day Russell found some scissors and evened out Amos's hair as best he could and found a hat for him to wear. In the afternoon they walked together into town and went to the library. Russell sat with the want ads while Amos wandered the aisles for an hour, picking up book after book and setting them back as gently as if they were eggs. The library had a cart with tattered paperbacks for twenty-five cents apiece. Russell counted out five dimes, and Amos spent another hour looking through the paperbacks for the two he wanted most. He finally chose them based largely on their lurid covers. Russell scanned each one and handed them back to Amos with a shrug. "Have to start somewhere," he said.

It was already growing dark when they left the library and strolled along the empty cruise ship docks. The hulking mountains that fenced the town were silhouetted against the dim gray sky. They left the docks and cut through town before heading back south down Thane. Amos chatted about the library, asked if they could go back tomorrow, what it took to get a check-out card. Russell considered the job situation. The want ads were a bust, but he figured it was time to stop treading water. He would catch the bus out to the job center. He would at least make an effort.

"How long does it take you to read a whole book?" Amos asked. They were on Main Street, heading toward the Crystal Palace. Russell could make out the usual small crowd of people in and around the bus shelter.

"Depends on the book," said Russell. "Depends on what else I'm doing."

"I'm going to read books all the time."

There was a clutch of smokers around the door of the Imperial. Russell and Amos stepped off the sidewalk to move around them. "Well, you've got two. You're off to a good start," said Russell. He looked up absently as they passed the smokers and locked eyes with the man with the cauliflower ears from the bathroom.

"What are you looking at?"

Russell looked down and away but the man advanced out of the group. "What are you looking at, you piece of shit?"

Russell raised his hands, moving away into the street. The man advanced toward him quickly, flicking his cigarette at him and grabbing at his jacket, shaking him. "What are you doing here? Didn't I tell you to get out?" Russell leaned back, trying to pull away. He felt himself going limp. Then Amos was between them, shoving at the man, trying to break his grip on Russell. The man spun, knocking Amos in his face with an elbow, hurling him to the ground. Amos seemed to crumple and the man kicked him, making awkward contact against Amos's shins. Amos curled into a ball. Russell stood trembling, his hands yet raised in the air. The man cleared his throat loudly and spat, a wet smack landing in Amos's hair. For a moment everything was still. Then a voice came booming from the Crystal Palace.

"Hey, you."

Down the street came Fat George. Not running but coming fast—he seemed to almost float. His arms were outstretched in the pose of a mounted grizzly—his shirt was open, exposing his hairless belly. "Hey, you fuckers. I'm gonna eat your face."

The crowd of smokers tightened and pulled back. The cauliflower-eared man stood his ground. "Stay out of it, you drunk muck," he said.

"Haaa," roared Fat George, coming faster.

The cops were on Fat George before he could take a swing. They came at a flat run, utility belts jangling, and combined their momentum with Fat George's to spin him hard into the rough wall of the building. They cuffed him as a cruiser pulled to the curb. The crowd of smokers relaxed, observers again. Russell reached for Amos and pulled him to his feet. Blood from his nose smeared the boy's cheeks. Russell pulled him away from the crowd now watching the routine and unremarkable arrest of Fat George for drunk and disorderly conduct.

"My eyes are watering. I can't see," said Amos.

"Hang on to me," replied Russell. "I can see fine."

Two cops, each taking an arm, led Fat George off the sidewalk and leaned him against the cruiser. He looked back at the crowd. "I blue ticket *you*, motherfuckers. I am Wooshkeetaan, Wolf Eagle. Aak'w Kwáan Tlingit. And I blue ticket all you."

Russell looked back at Fat George as he led Amos away. Fat George nodded at him and called out to Amos. "You watch my tent, okay. You keep it good." Then he grinned to himself and raised his eyebrows at the cop standing next to him. "Hey, Officer Vandiver, you got real nice shoes on today."

By the time they reached camp, Amos's nose had stopped bleeding. They paused at a creek that cut through Thane Road in a culvert, and Russell wet a handkerchief and washed away the blood. Amos's face was swollen, and he did not speak. In the fight he had lost both the books.

Russell helped Amos into the tent. The boy curled into a ball and went silent. Russell made a fire and warmed a pan of powdered milk and brought it to Amos in a mug. "Drink this," he said. "You will feel better."

"Came here to be punished and ought to be punished," Amos whispered.

"No," said Russell. "Drink this and you will feel better."

Russell left the mug and backed out of the tent. He noticed the carved piece of wood wrapped in twine. He took it and stood, unwrapping the wolf roarer and letting it dangle. He went through the steps as Amos had done and began to swing it slowly over his head. He stood next to the tent in the light of the fire. He swung it until it sounded a pitch, a scream, a warning to the darkness. To keep the bears at bay.

the times of
danil garland

IF YOU PLANT BLUEGRASS YOU GET MUSIC, and if you plant dogwood you get barking, but if you plant roses all you get is roses, said Stevo the Gypsy. It was also Stevo the Gypsy who once said that there's only one way to tell whether a gun is loaded before pulling the trigger and blowing off most of his jaw, so he had to acknowledge that he was wrong about some things. "But I am not wrong about Tammy Barnes," he said. "That girl is a sex grenade." He waved his hand at all of us, his friends and acolytes gathered in his trailer. "Someone just has to pull the pin."

Our town lies in the fold of a map. It is small and many strange things happen, and each generation is allowed only one beautiful woman. Tammy Barnes was ours. Her family was Jehovah's Witness, so talking to her required ingenuity. I made my attempt in the autumn, hoisting a ladder to her window in the night and tapping the glass ever so softly in the hope that she would swing wide the casement and allow me to recite "Sonnet 116." My efforts roused their Labrador, and my fingers, frozen in the cold, lost their grip and I fell, catching and breaking my ankle in a rung of the ladder and pulling it down upon me with a crash. Her father, bewildered with sleep, fished me from the snow and drove me to the clinic. I recited the sonnet to him, and he said that I was a nice boy, but that I should engage in some serious self-reflection.

"Self-reflection is all well and good," said Stevo the Gypsy, "but what you really need is balls. And vision. And Carlos here has both." Carlos told us his plan to get with Tammy Barnes. He was joining the Jehovah's Witnesses, marching down to the Kingdom Hall the very next day. "He's putting his immortal soul on the line," said Stevo the Gypsy. "That's nuts of steel." I countered that it wasn't such a big deal, that Prince was a Jehovah's Witness. "You've had your chance, Shakespeare," said Stevo the Gypsy. "Don't gripe."

It was the time of the plane crashes, and that winter we were all busy clearing debris and hoarding treasure and finding new coats that fit our thin shoulders. We lost many of our leading citizens. We split our days between mourning and flea markets. Even so we found time to visit Stevo the Gypsy and drink his rusty tap water and wrestle each other on his ratty couch. All of us except for Carlos, who didn't come around anymore. I saw him once, months later in the parking lot of Foodland. He said he had become a publisher of the Kingdom, that he was headed to Uruguay to tell people there about the ransom paid by Jesus Christ and His heavenly rule on earth that began upon His return in 1914. He asked after Stevo the Gypsy and I told Carlos that he was running for mayor. "I suppose somebody has to," said Carlos. "But tell him from me that to participate in the affairs of government is to become an ally of Satan."

"I'll pass that along," I said. As Carlos turned toward the bus stop, I asked, "What about Tammy Barnes?"

Carlos grinned. "Dude, she's been engaged since she was sixteen."

Stevo the Gypsy said Carlos was a rose, that he couldn't be anything else no matter what. "But you," he said, grabbing me by the shoulder, squeezing his fingers through the down of my new coat, "you are a lupine, and if you plant a lupine you get a wolf." Stevo the Gypsy said that when he was mayor that we would plant only flowers of action and flowers that could tell time, like morning glory and evening primrose. That we would then destroy all of the clocks and live again like free men. We would take the lids off of the garbage cans and let the bears eat like kings. We would train every citizen in the art of self-deception to protect them from injury.

"But what will you do about love?" I asked. "And its impediments?"

"Politics has no answer to that question," he said. "Horticulture neither."

Then it was the time of gathering signatures. We stood in the parking lot of Foodland and other auspicious places along the bus route, and sometimes Stevo the Gypsy would join us, looking frowzy and shattered with his Jolly Roger T-shirt and ragged jaw. Even without him around no one would sign his nomination list, and thus we all felt contemptible and low. I didn't recognize anyone in my town anymore. Everyone had left or died and had given their places to strangers and cripples. Only the ravens were the same, hunched and croaking in the drizzle like witnesses against us.

When I quit the campaign Stevo the Gypsy said, "You have become an impediment to my rule on earth."

I said, "Jesus Christ returned to begin His rule in 1914."

"Well," Stevo the Gypsy said, "He's done fuck-all since."

What followed was the time of fishing. I left town on a power troller that ported out of Elfin Cove, a village haunted by Kushtaka and residential fires. My captain believed in Satan and for sport made me ascend and descend the boat ladder even on the coldest of days. My fingers froze, but I never fell and broke my ankle, and I never recited for him a sonnet. I engaged in serious self-reflection. I kept my mouth shut and caught salmon. I became a fisher of fish. Humpies and dogs, but also money fish: kings and reds and cohos. I ran the girdies and dressed the monies as they came gasping from the sea, flicking with my knife the pyramid-shaped hearts of the kings onto the deck for the captain's toddler daughter to eat raw and grinning as the boat heaved in the swell.

Dog salmon have big flat eyes that come at you like bubbles from the drain of a water fountain. They have no scent at all. King salmon smell like metal, like a wet gun barrel, and they have the jaws of a wolf. But a coho, fresh caught and muscling in your arms, its scales flashing silver and rose in the sun, smells like a garden, like new-cut grass.

We fished the same drag off of Cape Spencer until our lips cracked and bled and the toddler became her generation's beautiful woman. Many boys drowned in the sea trying to reach her. From the deck I could hear them wheezing out snatches of poetry until they were swallowed by the waves or shouted down by the screeching gulls.

The time of the plane crashes returned. Will Rogers and Ted Stevens died. Hale Boggs and Nick Begich disappeared into a fold in the map. I kept to the sea and missed the mourning and the flea markets and pulled my jacket close around my shoulders against the wind that grew ever more bitter.

Eventually we are all Time's fool. I heard that Stevo the Gypsy moved to Coeur d'Alene. I heard that Carlos was hit by a car in Montevideo. I heard that Tammy Barnes had two kids. In the daylight I can't remember their faces, but they come at me like knives in the night. Then I lie awake and listen to the humpbacks moaning in the murk below and wonder, after we die and our mark is ever-fixed in the earth, what gardens will remain and what flowers we finally become.

dendromancy

MOST PROBLEMS BEGIN AS SOLUTIONS. Kudzu started as a solution for soil erosion. DDT started as a solution for mosquitoes. Thalidomide began as a solution to morning sickness. The first-order problem seems so intractable, so insurmountable, that the gamble of fixing it disarms rational thought. Anything to scratch an itch. Only when the pencil-end snaps beneath the cast, or one's field clots with vines, does perspective return and the second-order problem manifests. An itch is one thing; birth defects are another. I once heard of a man who survived a suicide attempt off the Golden Gate Bridge. At the moment of launch, during the weightless pause before he plummeted toward the sea, he realized in a burst of clarity that all of his problems were petty except for just having jumped from the Golden Gate Bridge. In my case, the problem was that at eighteen I felt aimless, friendless, and alone. I suffered from a longing as vague and corrosive as nostalgia. The world I lived in was blurred and indistinct. I had no words for any of it. My solution was Cassie.

Cassie was a witch. And not the friendly Wiccan-earth-goddess-tattoo type who gives her children sweet-but-absurd names. Cassie was a straight-up Grimm's-fairy-tale witch. She was a strict Manichean who believed in good and evil: black and white. She had decided to play for the winning team, and so dressed in black. She and her friends came into the coffee shop in downtown Juneau where I worked, and she drank the same tea I liked: Market Spice—the Seattle kind with the flavored fob—the thin square of cardboard at the end of the teabag string. Placed on your tongue, like a wafer, the fob burned your mouth with cinnamon oil. Sometimes having only one thing in common gets you started with someone. Cassie told me I had sweet eyes. She made me a mix tape of bleak music. I had never been picked for any team. I would have followed her anywhere.

Cassie told us that the original human sin was consciousness. That God had forced the Fall with His insistence that Adam name the animals. That the serpent had nothing to do with it. "Animals live in the world like water in water," Cassie said. "We do not." We are estranged from the world we have named, and the naming is why we are lonely. Dominion is the unbearable condition, she explained, not a gift. Our task was to recover our birthright and move in the world as indivisibly as the wolf that eats the caribou or the caribou that is eaten by the wolf. "Like water in water," she said.

Only after Cassie and her friends, who had become my friends, killed Dylan Hamner, one of our friends, and ate slices of his heart by the light of a pallet bonfire, did my second-order problem become manifest. Certainly I had been there; I was the one with a car. A Buick Skylark. It could hold all seven of us. Dylan said he didn't mind being a caribou if that's what it took for us to become wolves. Even within our mopey circle, Dylan was notable for his despair. He had sweet eyes.

We drove that night across the bridge to Douglas Island and then north to Outer Point, where an edge of the gray Pacific huffed and seethed through the pores of a black-cobbled beach. But while Cassie drowned Dylan in the sea and made him water in water, I wandered from the beach into the woods. I didn't follow any trail; I just pushed through the thicket and into the forest. Alone in the darkness, I placed my hand on the rough bark of a looming tree and felt the adhesive grab of sap upon my palm. The name of the thing I touched, Sitka spruce, *Picea sitchensis*, came unbidden to my tongue. I remembered in a flood the rangy red-bearded man at the Boy Scout camp, ten years before, who taught us the name, who had each of us touch the tree in turn and repeat the name after him. Now, the words burned a furrow behind my eyes. Everything has a name: longing, murder, trees. Names have edges that cannot blur, and we are obliged to say them. There is a reverb between the touching and the naming that we must weather. I felt a great vertigo and retched from the shaking of it.

I think about that moment all of the time now. Not the killing. I feel bad about Dylan and the violence against his body, whether he wanted to be a caribou or not. I am sorry for the Hamners. But I think now about the spruce and its name and the intimate distance that naming enforces. Some days in the LCCC yard, when the sun slants right against the forest on the rising flanks of Thunder

Mountain beyond the flashing razorwire, I feel the furrow burn again. Always it is fleeting. Often it is not there at all. Some summers I catch the upward spiraling call of a Swainson's thrush. And I tell the sullen fellas marking their shuffled time that it is a Swainson's thrush they hear. That's its name, I say. Listen, I say. It has two voice boxes, I say. It sings two songs at once. That's why it is so beautiful.

bridge to nowhere

WARREN BELL SHOWED UP ON MY PORCH at six in the morning and pushed his moon face to the window from the darkness outside. I was on the phone, a long-distance interview for a law job in Atlanta. He waved a piece of paper at me as though it was something significant. I waved back at him, pointing at the phone, signaling him to leave. He nodded and waddled out of view, tucking the paper into his jacket pocket. Warren lived in an apartment across the street. I'd never really been kind to him, but I knew he'd come back.

The interview wasn't going well. I'd applied to three jobs in my initial panic after getting fired, and two had already said no. The Atlanta job felt like my last boat out of town, and I couldn't miss it. I'd let myself imagine leaving Alaska, starting over somewhere new and uncomplicated. If the Atlanta job didn't pan out, I didn't know what I'd do. The average white American male supposedly lives to be seventy-five. At thirty-two, it seemed like more time than I could handle.

The interviewer asked me what, in my opinion, my weaknesses were. I paused before answering, took a sip of coffee. I'd considered that question a fair amount, given how things had unfolded. My weaknesses were, in my opinion, that I was longwinded in conversation, lackadaisical in my work, and unreliable in most situations. I had a reputation for agreeing to do things and then failing to do them. I was given to daydreaming and, as my ex-wife was fond of pointing out, impotence. I was a liar and a drunk and a spendthrift. A confluence of flaws that left me divorced, unemployed, friendless, sitting in my bathrobe in the dark at six in the morning in Juneau, Alaska, interviewing for a job that I needed but had little chance of getting. The distance between who I imagined myself to be and who I had become seemed to widen daily, leaving a gulf that filled me with dread.

It was 10:00 a.m. in Atlanta. Light and warm, probably. I envisioned the hiring committee sitting in suits at a long table in a conference room with a speakerphone in the center. I heard them clearing their throats, shuffling papers, whispering. The noises echoed across the cavernous phone line. Voices separated by four thousand miles. "Ron?" the woman asked. "Did you hear that last question?"

"Sure," I said, taking another sip of coffee. "My weaknesses. I can get a bit too obsessive over the details, and I sometimes find it hard to delegate."

"Okay," she said. "Thank you. Any other questions for Mr. Bunt?" There was a long pause.

"I'm just curious to hear what Alaska's like," someone said, his soft Southern accent bending his vowels.

I looked out the window. Dark and wet and grim. A small gray city, isolated at the ass-end of the world, besieged by rain and booze and disappointment. My hometown. A place I expected everything from and which probably expected more of me. "I grew up here," I said. "So I'm used to it. It's probably just like anyplace else."

After the interview, I unplugged the phone and made another pot of coffee. I poured some whiskey in my mug and waited for Warren.

Warren lived across the street, on the downhill side of Gastineau Avenue, in a crumbling moss-covered apartment building. My rented house, an old miner's shack, was on the uphill side. Gastineau Avenue was a seedy dead end at the foot of Mount Roberts, just above downtown. People drove fast on it even though it didn't go anywhere— tearing up and down the narrow street at forty or fifty miles an hour. Warren hated that.

I moved to Gastineau in October, just after the split. Jessica fought to keep the house out by Twin Lakes, close to her work at the hospital. I said I didn't care at the time. I wanted to live downtown anyway, close to the law firm where I was an associate and walking distance to the bars. From my porch I could see across to Douglas Island, connected to the mainland by a short bridge. The hillsides of Douglas are gashed with dreary brown condominiums, built in the late seventies. I grew up in one. Most days the island of my childhood was obscured by fog or low clouds. I preferred it that way.

I met Warren the day I moved in. He was on the sidewalk when I drove past him, yelling and waving his arms at me. I almost hit him. I braked in the middle of the street to see if he was all right, to see what the hell he wanted. Warren was short and heavyset, probably my age but it was hard to tell. He wore a thick blue down parka that swished when he moved his arms. His round face seemed almost childlike. He had thick glasses with black plastic frames that slid down his small, flat nose. He backed away when I got out of my car. I was in a foul mood and it showed.

I asked if he was okay. He held out his hands, palms together. They were trembling. His ears were red with cold. "There's no sign here yet," he said. "For the speed limit."

"Why were you screaming at me?"

"I didn't. I just was talking loud because you were in your car. I was just saying to remind you to slow down. To drive slow."

It took a moment for me to register that there was something off about him. Something in his manner, his speech, that suggested he wasn't quite right. Simple maybe. I took a breath. The cold air prickled inside my nose.

"It's just there are animals around," he continued. "Cats and dogs. Porcupines. Bears even. You can't see them if you drive fast. You'll hit them. Lots of people do. I say to slow down until the city puts up a sign. I've been saying to put up a sign, but they don't." So that was Warren. Sometimes he would wheeze on a silver harmonica to pass the time, no tunes, just making chords of his breath in and out. He nodded at slow cars, shouted at speeders, and officiated over the occasional animal his efforts failed to protect.

I still worked at the firm the first few months I lived on Gastineau, and Warren took an interest in me right away. He noticed my suit, found out that I was a lawyer, and wanted to show me his letters to the city about the sign. They were all printed in his loopy scrawl on blue-lined paper: painstaking compositions that told of the speeding, of the narrow street, with dates and times of the speeders, of the animals run over and their stories. There was an orange cat crushed beneath a Toyota Tacoma in August. The owner, a thin woman who lived in the same apartment building as Warren, wept at the spot, still in her nightdress. A familiar three-legged stray dog killed in March. A porcupine smashed by a Subaru Outback. The letters received no meaningful response. Warren made a sign of his own from cardboard, 10 MPH PLS spelled out in strips of duct tape. The sign lasted a few days before the cardboard buckled in the rain and the tape sloughed off, flapping like thick tinsel in the wind. Warren seemed undaunted. I could usually hear him wheezing on his harmonica, shouting his warnings. Perhaps the paper he'd been waving through the window was finally an answer.

I poured some more coffee and added another slug of whiskey. The thin, watery light of dawn filtered through the clouds. It was April, and getting lighter earlier. Spring was coming but slowly. An extra minute of daylight tacked on like a meager tip after a lousy meal.

I heard someone climbing my stairs, and then the heavy tread of Warren's shoes on my deck. Warren's face appeared again. He waved the paper, grinning. I secured my bathrobe and opened the door.

"I got a plan, buddy," said Warren as he pushed in. I sat on the couch, a threadbare floral number, and motioned to the rickety chair across from me. "Have a seat and tell me about it."

"I'm gonna stand while I tell you."

He stepped quickly toward me and dropped the paper in my lap with a flourish, then stepped back, nodding, as though to give me the space I needed to comprehend it. I put down my coffee and unfolded the paper. It was a property tax bill, past due, for twelve hundred dollars. The taxed property was a lot number on Glacier Highway.

"I didn't know you had property," I said.

Warren nodded. "Yeah, I do. My folks left it to me. My mom did. I never go out there. But you see what I'm thinking, right?"

"Not really."

"I thought of it last night. When I was going to sleep. Right when you are going to sleep, you think of things. And I thought, well if the city wants me to pay, how about I say that I won't without a sign?"

"This is already past due."

"So they really want the money. So they'll do it."

I set the bill down on the table and retrieved my coffee. "If you don't pay the bill, they'll just put a lien on the property. The city won't haggle about it. The sign is a separate issue."

"We could try. Just mention it in a letter. Like," he dropped his voice, letting his fleshy lower lip protrude, "No money. No sign."

"I doubt that would work." Warren's face fell. "But the city pays attention to property owners," I said, in an effort to ease his disappointment, "so mentioning it might help. Where's this lot?"

Warren shrugged. "It's out the road. Past Tee Harbor. It's just land going up the hill, nothing on it. I never go there."

"Why not?"

He shrugged again. "Don't want to ride the bus all the way out there. It's three transfers. Takes all day. It's no good if you don't drive."

"Hell, we can go out and look at it now, if you want." I hadn't been outside for a while and the prospect was appealing. Perhaps the interview hadn't gone as bad as I thought. I deserved a day off. "I'll drive us out there."

Warren seemed unsure. "Now?"

"I'll get dressed. We can catch breakfast at Henry's."

He hesitated, rubbing the flat pad of his thumb on his nose, then smiled. "Sure thing, buddy."

I found a wrinkled shirt and a pair of jeans that didn't smell too bad. I splashed some water on my face and considered brushing my teeth but decided to skip it. The small things had become tiresome. Warren wouldn't notice or care. I brought a go-cup of coffee with a jigger of whiskey in it for the road.

The rain was heavy downtown but it cleared as we drove north. Once we passed through Mendenhall Valley and skirted around Auke Bay, the sky became blue. Past the ferry terminal Glacier Highway opens up along the coast. You can see across Stephens Passage to the Mansfield Peninsula, the northern tip of Admiralty Island. Once you pass Lena Point you can see across Favorite Channel to Shelter Island and in the distance behind see the towering peaks of the Chilkat Range. Place names I studied on a map when I was homesick in college. On a map, the islands of the Alexander Archipelago are like puzzle pieces spread out on the gray-green carpet of the North Pacific Ocean. Everything that was once connected when the world was young. Slowly drifting apart now, separated by great distances.

I slowed on the dangerous curve just past the turnoff for the local college and picked up speed again around De Hart's, the last convenience store out the road. We started to pass large houses: mansions designed on log cabin themes, walls of windows facing the sea. Rich people moving in from god knows where and driving up the cost of land. The city had been busy updating the assessments.

"You know," I said, "at the city's mill rate, they're valuing your property at nearly ninety grand. It's probably worth even more. A hundred, maybe. Did you know that? You've got some money. How long have you been paying taxes on that place?"

Warren pursed his lips in thought. "Mom died eleven years ago. She left some money for the taxes that got paid by Mr. Hugo. I got a bill last year and he said that the tax money was gone and I had to pay it. It wasn't much, not as much as this year."

"Hell," I said, "you could sell it. Go on vacation. Buy a place of your own downtown. Move out of that crap apartment."

Warren shrugged. "I like Gastineau. It's a good place. Everything I need. Except there's no sign."

"A vacation then. Mexico, Hawaii, Thailand. Someplace warm. You could get a tan. How long has it been since you had a tan, Warren?"

He snickered. "Me, with a tan." He shook his head. "In a bathing suit with a tan." He snickered again and then he said, "You know where I'd like to go?" He shifted toward me. "I want to go to Iceland."

"Iceland?" I asked. "You live in Alaska. It's the same thing."

"Iceland's different, buddy. I saw *National Geographic* pictures. They heat their homes with volcanoes."

"Okay," I laughed. "Just give me the extra and I'll fly to Mexico. I need a tan."

Warren grinned. "Sure thing, buddy." We passed the Shrine of Saint Therese, passed Eagle River where the land goes flat and alluvial, spread with silt from the mountain glaciers.

"So where exactly are we going?" I asked.

"Just a bit more," he said. "Just a little farther. I'll tell you."

My hands felt light on the wheel. The day was warming some in the sunshine. There was a softness to the air, a fleeting scent of spring that made my chest ache. I thought about Mexico, a trip Jessica and I had taken one winter. Days spent on the beach, burning in the sun. The translucent geckos skittering on the walls of our hotel room at night. Back when the jigsaw-puzzle pieces of our lives fit together as a couple, forming a fine interlocking picture of us and our house and our car, with ample room for dogs and children. But even then ragged gray cardboard showed on the edges of pieces I'd muscled into place, leaving small gaps between us that only grew wider, giving her room to leave.

The road slid away from the coast, into the enclosure of the dark spruce and hemlock forest. Warren leaned forward intently as we drove, mouthing silent words. He told me to slow down. We crept along for nearly another mile. The tires hummed loudly as we passed over a short trestle bridge and then went back up onto the asphalt.

"Here," he said, finally. "Stop here."

I pulled off onto the sloping gravel shoulder of the road. I asked if he was sure. He nodded vigorously and I cut the engine. There was a pullout about twenty yards ahead with an old truck parked on it, but I decided to leave my car where it was.

"Well," I said, "let's take a look."

There was a muddy path evident above the bank of the shoulder. A track cut through the hedge of devil's club, threading uphill into the gloom between the spruce. Warren seemed confused when he saw the path, gesturing vaguely in another direction, but we stepped up on it, following the lightning-bolt impressions left by someone's Xtratuf boots. As we climbed I remembered why I wanted to return to Juneau after law school in the first place. Between the trees were needle-coated humps of emerald moss and the yellow shoots of early skunk cabbage. The spicy scent of soil and damp. A thrush was singing a climbing series of flutelike notes. The reddish new branches of blueberry bushes pushed up into the shafts of light allowed by the wide flat leaves of devil's club. I could see shoots of twisted stalk, whose watermelon-like berries I gorged on as a child even though too many caused the shits. All of this I still loved, but it seemed remote from me now. I picked a leaf of twisted stalk. I placed it in my mouth and it was bitter on my tongue.

The trail continued steeply uphill. We were both winded after the initial stretch. The gnarled twistings of thick spruce roots broke the trail and made the going difficult. Neither of us wore boots. My shoes were soaked. Warren was muddy to his knees, having slipped twice, landing heavily. We paused to catch our breath.

"Are you sure," I asked, "that this is your property?"

"It feels different," said Warren. He looked around, as though lost, but then he said, "That's the nose tree. I remember it." He turned to me. "I remember it." Warren pointed at a massive spruce with a branch broken near its trunk, leaving a hump vaguely resembling a nose. Not particularly distinctive, but I nodded and we pressed on.

About seventy yards above the road we came upon a tidy wood-pile, covered with a black tarp. I was concentrating on my feet to be sure where to step, but the tarp caught my eye. When Warren saw it a look of concern flickered over his face. The trail curved ahead of us and we followed it into a small clearing where there was a domed, tent-like structure, some twenty feet across. It sat atop a round wooden platform several feet above the ground. It looked like the top of a grain silo, sliced off and dropped into the forest.

"What is that?" asked Warren.

"It's a yurt," I answered.

"What's it here for?"

A silver stovepipe stuck from the side of the yurt, and a thin stream of white smoke curled into the air. "Someone's home," I said. "Let's ask."

I stepped up the wooden stairs to the door and knocked. Warren stood a few paces off, looking bewildered. There was no response, so I knocked again. I heard voices inside. I turned to Warren and nodded. "They're home." He stared back at me, breathing heavily through his mouth.

The door opened. It was a young woman, maybe twenty-four. Her long blonde hair was disheveled and her face was flushed with sleep; the marks of a blanket creased her cheek. She wore an Alaska Folk Festival T-shirt and shearling slippers. Even half awake she was pretty. I suddenly wished that I had brushed my teeth.

"What do you want?" she asked. A man's voice, muffled, asked her who it was. She turned back to us. "Who are you?" she asked.

"My name is Ron Bunt," I said. "I'm a lawyer. And he," I turned, "is Warren Bell. The owner of this land." I raised my eyebrows slightly for effect. "And now may I ask who you are?"

"Oh," said the woman. She turned away, keeping her right hand on the door. "Ish," she called. "It's some lawyer about the property." She looked back at me and pushed the door until it almost closed but did not latch.

Warren called up to me. "Who are these people? What are they doing here?" I stepped back down and stood next him.

"I don't know," I said. "Hippies of some sort. Squatters. We'll work it out."

The door opened again and a man stepped onto the porch. He was tall and thin and handsome, wearing faded blue jeans and no shoes. His shirt was open and unbuttoned, exposing a strong chest and a stomach as flat as a shark's. He had dark hair and a sparse beard and keen blue eyes. I disliked him instantly.

"What do you want?" he said. His voice was nonchalant, a smile played on his lips.

I introduced myself again, placing special emphasis on my credentials, and then introduced Warren. "It seems that you are squatting on his land," I said, as though it was an impartial but shattering diagnosis of the situation. His cocky half smile did not shift.

"Actually," he replied in a slow voice, "you're trespassing on mine." His voice was soft, with a faint Southern accent. It reminded me of the voices I'd heard that morning on the call to Atlanta.

"I'm not trespassing," said Warren, agitated and loud. His parka swished as he moved his arms. "You're the ones trespassing."

I motioned for Warren to calm himself. "This seems pretty simple to me," I said, maintaining my lawyer voice, analytical and dispassionate. "You thought this land was open, so you made the best of it. But now you know that the land is fully claimed by its owner, and I'm sure that we can give you a reasonable time to vacate the premises." I turned back to Warren and nodded reasonably. He stared at me blankly for a moment and then nodded reasonably, too.

The man crossed his arms. "It might have been simple a while back," he said. "But I've been here for over nine years. Open, notorious, and hostile. If you're really a lawyer, you understand what I'm saying." He let his eyes linger on my muddy shoes and unshaven face, on Warren's plump and dirty figure, and then shrugged.

"What is he talking about?" asked Warren, his voice pitching high and confused. "What is he talking about, hostile?"

I paused a moment to collect my thoughts. "He appears to be claiming," I said rather loudly, showing off for the woman inside, "that he has a case for adverse possession. But it's not quite that easy from the point of view of the law." This was a bluff. I didn't know much about adverse possession, just snippets from first-year property class. I'd never heard of it actually happening but for fences and minor property-line disputes, the odd corner of a building. Never a whole house or yurt or whatever it was.

"I don't appear to be doing anything." The man maintained his even tone. "I've done it. I have all the documentation. Friends come and visit us here. The neighbors know it's ours. We had a mailbox up for seven years until we got a P.O. box. I've talked to a lawyer myself. We can sue you for quiet title if we want. Or you can sign a quitclaim deed. It doesn't matter to me."

"What lawyer did you talk to?" I asked.

"Josh Hughes, downtown."

"He's an idiot," I said, lamely.

The man shrugged again. "If you don't protect your property, why should the law care about it?" He looked straight at Warren. "We've been here living here nine years, Mr. Bell. Never once saw you."

Warren's face reddened. "I never thought someone would come on it," he shouted. "This is my mother's land, and I never thought anybody'd come on it like you did."

The man watched Warren impassively. The curtain hanging in the yurt's window twitched. I put my hand on Warren's shoulder, turning him, steering him back down the trail. He kept looking over his shoulder at the man watching us, stumbling as I pushed him along. "It's okay, Warren," I said. "Let's get out of here for now."

The trail was easier going down. In less than five minutes we were back in my car heading south down Glacier Highway, toward town. Warren seemed dazed. He stared into his lap, focusing on his clenched hands, lower lip protruding. "I'm hungry," I said. "Let's go to Henry's and get some lunch. We can talk it over there." Warren gave a slight nod.

As we drove I thought about Josh Hughes. He was my age, from Ohio or somewhere in the Midwest, and had already made partner at his firm. He wasn't an idiot, and I was wrong to have said so. People liked him; he was polished in all the right ways. He worked hard and was responsible and made everything look easy and I resented him for it, as though he had taken the life I expected to lead. The life that was mine by right. Just for the wanting of it. I suspected he and his wife would buy an Auke Bay mansion soon enough.

At Henry's, Warren glanced around uncomfortably and said that he'd never been here before. In the bar there was a mechanical bull you could ride on weekends. I told Warren about it and he waddled off to see. I ordered a double Bloody Mary for me and a Pepsi for him.

When Warren came back a few minutes later he was grinning. "That's something," he said. "I sat on it. That sure is something. Did you ever ride it?"

I took a drink and shook my head no. The ice slid down the glass and hit my nose. I ordered another.

"We should sometime. We should come back here and ride it. You want to?"

I shrugged. "Sure."

Warren grinned again and studied his menu, swinging his legs around the bar stool like a child. "That'll be fun, buddy. We're having fun. You're a good friend."

I flinched, but Warren didn't notice. I didn't consider him a friend. Friends are peers. Warren was something else. An eccentric I humored. A weirdo I was noble enough to help. Someone low enough to look up to me.

Warren ordered a cheeseburger, onion rings, and a milkshake and thanked the waitress. I got an order of fries and switched to beer. I watched him eat. He was a messy eater, cramming burger and onion rings into his rubbery mouth, nodding as he chewed, as though he was keeping time to some secret music. It occurred to me that I knew something Josh Hughes didn't. I ordered another beer.

"Warren?" I asked, getting his attention. "Have you ever been tested? For IQ, and all that? Did they test you in school?"

He stopped chewing and stared at me, confused. He said no, the word muffled by the food in his mouth. He swallowed. "I'm not stupid. Why would you ask that, buddy?"

"Nothing," I said. "It's just I've got an idea about your property."

He shrugged. "I was thinking about that. I was mad but I don't really care. I don't ever go there."

"Well that's not the issue," I said. "It's your land. By right. You should be able to sell it, whatever. It's the principle of the thing. You could buy a mechanical bull of your own."

Warren chortled. "Nah. We can just come here and ride it when we want. I don't need one."

"In any event, I should talk to them again. I've got something I want to discuss. I won't let them push you around." There was no hurry. I had time to properly research the case law and organize my thoughts. There was no reason to talk to them if they were already represented and, if they were, I shouldn't talk to them at all. But I wanted to wear Hughes' easy smile. I wanted the woman with the long blonde hair to be in my eye. I deserved to have a few good things come my way.

Warren poked a straw into his milkshake. "Whatever you say, buddy."

I finished my beer and paid. I wanted to go home first so we drove back downtown. I changed and freshened up a bit. Warren waited on the porch. I brushed my teeth and put on some clean slacks and a button-up shirt. I packed my satchel with a notepad and some pens. I left my wet shoes by the door and laced up a pair of dusty hiking boots. I told Warren that I should see them alone, that it might be better if I did. He said no. "I'm sticking with you."

It was nearly six o'clock in the evening by the time we pulled off the road at the bottom of the trail. I told Warren to wait in the car, that I would come get him if anything changed. He nodded. I gave him the keys. "I can't drive," he said. "You can run the radio if you get bored," I told him. "I won't be long."

I climbed the trail, which seemed shorter now that I knew where it led. I could smell the wood smoke through the trees. When I knocked on the door, the man answered.

"You again?" he asked.

"I was hoping to talk to you about Mr. Bell," I said. "Can I come in?"

He paused for a moment and then nodded, leaving the door open as he stepped back. "Take off your boots," he said.

The yurt was cozy inside. A sleeping loft, a small kitchen, a low table with cushions around it, a guitar and a banjo leaning against a post, a fiddle hanging from a hook above them. There was a lot of fabric, velvet and brocade, giving splashes of color. The doors of the squat black cast-iron stove were open and the room was warm, almost hot. The woman was in the kitchen, stacking dirty plates into a plastic tub. She had changed into jeans and wore a beaded tunic with the sleeves pushed up to reveal thin and delicate arms. Her hair was back in a braid, and I could see her face more clearly than in the morning. I must have gaped because she flushed slightly, beautifully, and turned away, almost coy. Half a bottle of wine was on the counter. I took off my boots and dropped my satchel by the door. I introduced myself again and they did the same. The man's name was Ishmael. The woman was Stella.

Ishmael invited me to sit, so I dropped tailor-style on a hard silk-covered cushion across the low table from him. "We had some wine with dinner," said Stella. "Do you want a glass?"

"Sure," I said, taking it when she handed it to me, watching her as she stepped back to the dishes. "This is a nice place."

I meant it, too. Their home seemed peaceful and content. It occurred to me that they were doing something right, living in the woods. It was the sort of peace Jessica had wanted. Or maybe it was, I never really knew. I thought of my own damp and rundown apartment, and I felt a slight pang of jealousy. Who were these people, outsiders, to live like this?

"We like it," said Stella. "We've been working on it for years."

"I can see that," I said. "And I don't think Mr. Bell necessarily wants you to move, but we should discuss where things stand." I proceeded to tell them my impressions of Warren's disability, overstating it but not by much, and explained that a judge would likely find a disabled landowner needed more notice of adverse possession than the average owner. It was an issue of fairness. I talked for some time, and Stella refilled my glass when it was empty.

Ishmael listened quietly, taking in the information. Then he stood and took down a bottle of whiskey. As he unscrewed the cap he raised his eyebrows at me and I nodded. The news gave him pause and he had decided to make nice. He filled two glasses and came back to the table. "I thought there was something weird about him," he said finally. "I don't know. I'll talk it over with Hughes."

"Well," I took a drink, "like I said, I don't think it's a question of making you move. Warren would take a price for it, I'm sure. A fair price."

Ishmael poured two more shots and I sat back, not wanting to push the issue just yet. I had disliked him at first, but he now seemed like a reasonable guy, perhaps a bit guarded but not a complete jerk. I asked him where he was from and he seemed to bristle at the question.

"I've been in Alaska for a long while," he said.

"But where are you from?" I persisted.

"Grew up in North Carolina," he said.

"I thought so. I can hear an accent in there," I drained another shot. The room seemed to be getting warmer. "I'm considering taking a job in Atlanta," I said nonchalantly.

Ishmael left his glass empty, so I took the bottle and poured another short one for myself. "That's Georgia," he said.

I shrugged. "The Lower 48 is all the same to me."

Stella finished in the kitchen and sat down on a cushion between me and Ishmael. She had the last of the wine in her glass so I finished my whiskey and poured another to keep her company. I waved the neck of the bottle toward Ishmael, but he shook his head. I smiled at Stella, feeling warm and comfortable. She smiled back, showing a flash of startlingly white teeth. Her eyes looked directly into mine and something shuddered open inside me. My breath went ragged for a moment.

"So," said Stella. "What's up?" There was no hint of the South in her voice; it was smooth and slightly husky. She leaned forward to adjust her cushion and I caught a glimpse of her cleavage, a curve of breast. I felt a stirring in my pants which was a pleasant surprise. I couldn't remember the last time I had an actual erection.

"He's proposing that we buy our own land," said Ishmael.

"No, no," I shook my head. It felt loose and wobbly on my neck. "No, no. Ownership is in dispute. A cloud on the title. All I'm saying is fair price." I finished my whiskey. "Can't talk numbers now, but just, fair price. That makes more sense, considering the cost of a lawsuit. Something that Hughes might not tell you."

"He explained it to me pretty well, I think," said Ishmael. "Regardless of what you think of him."

"Well, he's not really an idiot," I said generously. "It's just he's pretty new to the state, still figuring it out. He's not a five-seven-four."

"A what?" Stella cut in.

"That's the first tree dig . . ." I heard myself slur and started over. "The first three digits of your social security number if you're born here. In Alaska."

"So you were born here?" she asked.

"Hell yes, I was. This is my hometown. Hughes is a newcomer." I nodded to myself, feeling the words flow effortlessly. "He's stuck on fantasy Alaska, not real Alaska where people live. He doesn't get it. What it's like for real people. No disrespect, but Alaska isn't just being a hippie and living in the woods. It's real people."

"Sure," said Ishmael slowly. "No disrespect. But I live in the woods, I'm a real person. I lead a real life. The one I choose to lead. I don't see your problem with it." He stared at me hard without any kindness in his face.

My shoulders felt loose and easy. I didn't care what he thought. "My problem is you think you're some kind of wilderness hippie and all, but you're stealing someone's land, an Alaskan's land. That's complete horseshit."

His hard expression didn't change, but he added his cocky little smile. "Tell that to the Tlingits," he said.

"You got no idea what you are talking about," I said.

"Neither do you," he answered.

I turned to Stella, leaning close to her. "You understand, don't you?" The room felt incredibly hot and spinning and all I could see were her large blue eyes looking into mine, with lashes that seemed to brush the walls. The moment of now became swollen around me. Suddenly I wanted to kiss her more than anything in the world.

Whether Ishmael was there or not. Simple as that. I leaned in toward her, or meant to, but instead I slipped off my cushion, falling backward. Everything was hot and I felt very heavy and like time had passed. I blinked and sat up and my lap was wet. The room was quiet and they were both looking at me. "Shit, I'm sorry," I said. "Did I spill?"

"No. You pissed yourself." Ishmael stood and leaned over me. "Leave now. Leave. Get the fuck out of here." Stella was up too, standing in the kitchen. Watching me with her arms crossed, a look of horror on her face.

I stood but the room spun and I fell heavily onto one knee. My face was hot and it was difficult to breathe. I could hear myself gasping as though from a great distance. I felt strong hands under my armpits and suddenly I was upright and through the door, down the steps, and in a heap on ground. Ishmael stood back from me, panting slightly. "Fuck," he said. "Get a grip. Don't come back here." The door closed and then opened again. My boots and my satchel landed near me with bouncing thuds. My cheek rested on a patch of moss and it was soft and fragrant.

I awoke in the darkness. My slacks were wet and cold and everything ached. I startled upright, frightened and unclear of where I was. Gradually the night resolved into shapes and shadows. I could see the yurt, its windows dark. I could see the glint of the stovepipe and the shape of the trees. I took a step and felt the sharp spike of a broken branch dig into my foot. I bent over and waved my hands until I found my boots and my satchel and then I stumbled down the trail.

I lost the trail twice in the dark, falling over roots, pitching into devil's club, the thorns burning my hands. I stumbled into a tree and held it tight as I heaved my stomach into the dirt. It seemed hours before I reached the car, sliding into the ditch and staggering up the shoulder to the road.

The windows of the car were steamed, clouded with condensation. I pulled the door open but the inside remained dark. I could see Warren's bulk on the passenger seat, pushed into the corner of the car, as though to make himself small. He was wearing his seatbelt. He shifted when he saw me.

"Ronald?" he asked. "Ronald? Is that you?" His voice shook, his face was slack and mottled. He had been crying. His nose was red and the skin below it was wet.

"Yeah," I said.

"Oh God," he said, the tremor in his voice increasing. "Oh God, buddy. I thought they killed you. I thought they killed you. I didn't know what to do."

I eased into the driver's seat and closed the door. "It's okay," I said. "It was nothing." The key was in the ignition. I put my foot on the brake and switched it forward. Nothing happened. Silence.

"I ran the radio," he said plaintively. "And the heat. And then it just stopped. I didn't do anything. I didn't mean to break it. It just stopped."

I slouched forward, pressing my forehead against the cold rubber of the steering wheel. I could smell the sharp scent of urine and sick coming off my clothes. For a moment I couldn't tell if my eyes were open or closed, such was the darkness around me, within me. Who will love me when I'm this? I opened my eyes and sat back.

"It's all right, Warren. Nothing is broken. The battery just ran down is all. Someone will come by. Give us a jump." I opened the door and walked to the front of the car and sat on the hood. After a moment I felt the car shift on its springs as Warren got out. I stood and crossed the road and he followed me. I walked to the trestle where the road crossed a creek and leaned against the cold box-steel railing. The creek ran to the ocean, cutting an alley through the forest. In the light of the rising moon I could see the shape of the forest descending to the sea below and the shining mountains of the Chilkat Range across Favorite Channel.

Warren came and stood next to me. I dropped my head and took a deep breath. "I'm really sorry, Warren." My face burned and my throat was tight and it was difficult to speak. "I am wretched," I said. My nose was full and dripping and I didn't care to wipe it. "Jesus. I am really sorry."

"Hey," said Warren, leaning against me, wrapping his arm around me. "Hey. It's okay, buddy. We're friends. Everything's gonna be okay."

We stood like that for a time, looking out between the trees in the silence, across the water. "I was thinking," said Warren finally, "there should be a bridge here, a long one. Like San Francisco but even longer. So we could walk across and go to those mountains."

I followed his gaze and looked up again to the Chilkats. For a moment I could see Warren's bridge arcing in the air. A high silver thread connecting remote things that will never be connected. The puzzle pieces joined by an arch that never sleeps. Warren's arm was tight around me, holding me up. I leaned into him. "Yes," I said. "Yes. That is a wonderful idea."

roost

THE RONSONS, HANK AND ROBERTA, made a mistake early in their marriage: they bought a painting of a chicken from a neighbor's yard sale. The painting was small and warping away from its ornate wooden frame. On the painting's cardboard backing was scrawled the artist's name, Ellen Merryman, and the title, *Mr. Rooster Chicken, 1972.* The painting itself was an oil portrait of a rooster's head. The rooster, Mr. Rooster Chicken, addressed the viewer directly, wearing his cockscomb brushed casually to one side.

Hank made a point of showing the painting to friends and family whenever they were entertaining and there was a lull in conversation. Sometimes he'd take it down and show them the crabbed lettering of the old woman who had painted it. "Mr. Rooster Chicken!" he'd crow, like it was the punch line to a priceless joke, and usually Roberta would laugh along with him, though not as hard or for as long.

Friends and family misread the Ronson's delight over the painting as a genuine appreciation for the chicken motif. Over time, over years of birthdays and anniversaries and several housewarmings, the chickens accumulated. Eventually their house became a cautionary tale in misleading home décor: the hen-and-rooster salt-and-pepper shaker set, the Foghorn Leghorn novelty clock above the oven range, the dinner plates decorated with a quilt-pattern of barnyard fowl, chicken wall plates over the light switches, chicken knickknacks and umbrella stands and calendars and collectible weathervanes that did not turn in the wind.

Roberta, a handsome and efficient woman, worked as the office manager of a small law firm in the center of town. Hank, a usually genial man, thickening about the waist now that he was in his mid-forties, taught English at the local college. By all outward indications their marriage was pleasant and unremarkable. They seemed both to be solid, dependable people. It was a surprise then, when Hank failed to show up for his classes. It took a day or two before one of his more ambitious students alerted the department to Professor Ronson's absence. The department chair, upon hearing the news, cast a delegating eye around the office and fixed it on Ethan Thurso. Ethan also taught English at the college, though at that particular moment he was sitting on the corner of the secretary's desk, chatting up Alina with a wide grin on his round face.

"Ethan," said the department chair. "Have you heard anything from Ronson?"

Ethan stood and smoothed his khakis. "No. Should I have?"

"Apparently he hasn't been coming in. Can you give him a call and see what's up? Maybe he's sick or something."

Ethan shrugged. "Sure." He dialed the Ronson's number from Alina's phone, leaning over her slightly. After several rings the answering machine clicked on: Hank's loud voice in a cartoon southern accent, "Nobody's home at the chicken ranch. Lay an egg at the tone." Ethan began speaking, but after a moment he heard the scrabble of the phone being lifted and then Hank's voice.

"Hey, Ethan. I'm sorry . . . I meant to call . . . I just didn't." Hank sounded ragged, almost hoarse.

"No problem. We were just worried. Everything okay?"

There was a long pause. Ethan could hear Hank breathing, and the scratch of the receiver being pressed against Hank's face. He coughed. "Berta left me," he said finally.

"Oh hell," said Ethan. "Jeez. I'm really sorry to hear that. Are you all right?"

There was another long pause, and Ethan felt a brief irritation with himself for asking a stupid question. But really, what else can one say? Alina rolled her chair away from the desk quietly and headed toward the office kitchenette. Ethan watched her go.

"Yeah," Hank's voice was tight. "Look, would you mind covering my classes? Just for a few days?"

"Of course," said Ethan. "Anything you need."

"I have all the notes and everything. Their assignments. It's all here. It should be easy. Do you want to come by and pick it up? Or I could . . ."

"No, no. I'll come by. It's no problem. I'll be by in a bit."

The Ronsons lived in a split-level ranch on a quiet cul-de-sac, not too far from the college. Ethan and his wife, Miriam, had been there

91

on a few occasions before, for parties or dinners when the Ronsons entertained. He and Hank were cordial, though not particularly close. The Ronsons did invite him to their last anniversary party though. He gave them a metal trivet in the shape of a Rhode Island Red. He remembered Miriam chiding him for not buying something wood. He and Miriam had been married less than a year at the time, but she knew by heart the conventions of anniversary gifting.

It took a moment for Hank to answer the door after Ethan knocked. He was barefoot, dressed in baggy sweatpants and a buffalo plaid flannel shirt. His face was dark and unshaven, circles under his eyes. Seeing him thus, in the grace afforded by his suffering, Ethan adopted the slack, supportive face of a mourner who is not well acquainted with the deceased but who wants to be polite.

"Hey, Ethan. Thanks for coming by. C'mon in." Hank led the way down into the sunken living room and sat on the couch, hitching up his pants. The house was not especially large, but it was open. From the living room it was up three burgundy carpeted steps to the kitchen which led into the unused formal dining room which opened to the entryway which was en suite to the living room. If someone was chasing you through the house you could run endless circles without ever confronting a closed door.

"How's Miriam?"

"Good, good," said Ethan. "She's taken up Tai Chi. She's good."

"Good," said Hank significantly, seeming to protrude his eyeballs slightly with meaning. "You two are just starting out. That's good."

"I'm really sorry to hear about Roberta."

"Well . . ."

"No really. I'm sorry. That's tough."

Hank nodded and waved a dismissive hand in the air, as though to indicate the mention of a trifle. "Not much of a martial art, is it? For fighting. Tai Chi."

"No," said Ethan loudly, his back straightening brightly. He had expected to need the mournful expression longer, but now he dropped it and smiled easily. "I don't suspect it is. Perhaps it's effective only if your opponent is also using Tai Chi." Hank was silent. Ethan lowered his voice again, slackening his face. "Anyway. It must be tough. How are you feeling?"

Hank cleared his throat and pursed his lips, and then his mouth twisted as though he was doing something energetic and determined with his tongue. He scratched his head violently and a section of his hair stood on end. He cleared his throat again. "Well you know, Ethan," said Hank, "I feel a little pissed right now."

Ethan was taken slightly aback. He cleared his own throat. "I don't blame you," he said tentatively. There followed a long pause and he felt suddenly uncomfortable so he stood and turned his attention to a narrow bookcase crammed with knickknacks. He reached for a large wooden nesting doll, in the style of a Russian Matryoshka. It was in the usual squat shape but painted with the design of a chicken. "This is something," he said, turning to Hank. "New?"

"Alina gave that to us. To me."

"The secretary? Our office assistant? She gave this to you?"

"Yes."

"With the décolletage . . . ?"

"Yes."

". . . with the . . . ?"

"Yes."

Ethan realized that he was blurting. He reddened slightly. "She's nice," he said.

93

Hank nodded and exhaled loudly through his nostrils.

"Have you unpacked it?" Ethan asked. He mimed pulling the halves of the doll apart. "Is it chickens all the way down?"

"In the center there's an egg." Hank brushed his hair back and tugged on his pants. "A little wooden egg."

"Nice," said Ethan. "That's something." He returned to his seat and set the doll down on the coffee table between them. He leaned back in the chair and cupped his chin in his hand, attempting a return to the pose of an active and sympathetic listener.

"Do you want to talk about it? You don't have to. But it might help."

Hank sighed and did the mouth thing again. "She went for this conference in Reno. Some law firm administrator convention or something. She was only supposed to be gone four days, but she sent me a letter saying that she wasn't coming back. That she was taking a leave from work and that I would be contacted about the divorce. That it was nothing personal. Simple as that."

"Jesus. That's awful. And in Reno? Jesus. She didn't give any explanation or anything? Just nothing personal? That's a ridiculous thing to say."

"She sent me a poem, too. Neruda, of all people."

"Neruda?"

"The one about weariness. Where he says he is weary of the sea, and the earth." Hank rubbed his head again. "And weary of chickens."

"Oh yeah," said Ethan, nodding. "Good poem." He saw Hank grimace slightly and stopped short. "But really," he modulated his tone, adding umbrage, "it hardly seems appropriate. Christ. Nothing personal? What is that supposed to mean?"

"I really don't know." Hank's voice was ragged and hoarse again, almost a whisper.

Ethan sat quietly for a moment, allowing the silence to rest in the still room. Then he asked, "Do you want a drink or something? Do you have anything?"

"Sure," said Hank. "There should be some whiskey in the kitchen. In the cabinet above the fridge. I could do with a drink." He started to shift out of his slouch, leaning forward. "I'll get it."

"No, no," said Ethan, standing quickly. "You sit. I can get it."

Ethan stepped up the burgundy steps into the kitchen and found the whiskey. He found two tumblers amidst the pile of dishes in the sink and rinsed them. He shook each glass reasonably dry with sharp flicks of his wrist as he looked out the window above the sink into the Ronson's backyard. The yard was enclosed with a high wooden fence and one section of it, about a quarter, was fenced with chicken wire. A few scraggly black-and-white mottled hens scratched in the dirt or wandered aimlessly in and out of a hutch. Ethan paused and watched the chickens for a moment. He had never noticed a coop in the yard before, and it seemed to him that it was new. It made him uneasy, somehow. It was a step too far. He poured the drinks and carried them back into the living room, where Hank had returned to his slouch, staring blankly at the floor.

They drank for a time in silence, not looking at each other. Hank stared at the floor and Ethan stared at the wooden doll standing on the coffee table. Ethan fidgeted and decided to get some ice so he went back to the kitchen and refreshed both their drinks and then sat again. Finally Hank spoke.

"I really don't know why she left. I've been racking my brains about it. There was a lawyer at the firm, a kind of smarmy guy who tried to flirt with her. But I don't think she was having an affair. Why would she be having an affair?"

Ethan shrugged sympathetically. "Why does anyone do anything?"

"You think she was having an affair?" Hank's voice sharpened and his eyes became briefly narrow and beady. "You think I'm a cuckold?"

"Of course not," Ethan stammered. "I don't know anything, how would I? I was just saying that people are mysterious. You know that. I mean, think of Isabel Archer. Why does she go back to Osmond? Or Miss Brodie? There are limits to our knowledge. Our motives are hidden, sometimes even to ourselves, and no explanation really fits. It's like," continued Ethan, gesturing to the doll, with his glass, "why did the chicken cross the road? You know?"

Hank scowled. "Is that supposed to be funny?"

"No. I'm serious." Ethan felt the thrill of his idea rise within him, like a head of steam, pleasurable, pressing him on. "Why do you *think* Roberta left you?"

"I don't know." Hank's expression was sour. "Bored? Tired, maybe. Sick of her life?"

"To get to the other side?" Ethan spoke emphatically, as though he was teaching his students, trying to shake them into an appreciation of mystery.

"That's not funny, Ethan."

"I know. I'm not trying to be. But listen," he continued, "it's a philosophical question, don't you think? The chicken and the road. It's insoluble. The reasons never satisfy, they never kill the joke. It just goes on and on because motivations are mysterious. Why did the chicken cross the road? Why do people do what they do? Every answer fails." Ethan sipped on his drink. "Do you remember how funny that used to be? How funny that is to kids?"

"I don't really feel like talking philosophy right now."

"Sure. But isn't it interesting that no matter what the answer is, it never solves the mystery? The answer, no matter what it is, never stops you from asking the question again. That's why that joke sticks around. That's all I'm saying."

Hank took a deep breath and exhaled slowly. He took a sip of his drink and then set it down. He scratched the stubble on his cheek and leveled his eyes directly at Ethan. "Real people have their reasons," he said. "I never liked Henry James. Or Muriel Spark. And I never thought chicken crossing the road jokes were funny, actually. Unamusing."

A silence hung in the air. Ethan felt his enthusiasm dissipate, leaving him flushed and uncomfortable. He held his glass, cold with melting ice, briefly to his forehead and surreptitiously checked his watch. His stomach grumbled.

The silence was broken by the ringing of the phone in the kitchen. Hank glowered and didn't move to answer it. They sat, listening to the rings, anticipating each one. After a moment the answering machine clicked on, and Hank's recorded greeting echoed out. "Nobody's home at the chicken ranch. Lay an egg at the tone." A voice announced itself as a friendly reminder from Blockbuster.

Hank took a long sip of his drink and then sighed. "That recording doesn't seem funny anymore."

Ethan pursed his lips and felt a twinge of vindication. "I don't think it ever was, actually." He tried to cover himself with an ingratiating smile.

Hank stared at Ethan for a moment, his eyes beady again. Then he flapped a hand dismissively. "It was all supposed to be ironic. It was never because I *liked* chickens for Christ's sake." Hank stood suddenly and walked to the wall where the painting hung still. "Mr. Rooster Chicken, the whole thing. It was ironic," he said quietly.

"But now you've got actual chickens, Hank. It stops being ironic when you get actual chickens." Ethan finished his drink and set the glass down on the coffee table. He stood and joined Hank in front of the painting. In a house full of collectables, knickknacks, bric-a-brac, and tchotchkes, Mr. Rooster Chicken was the original. Like the single dollar bill pasted to the wall behind the counter of a diner, the antecedent and progenitor of the occult increase leading to the booths, the menus, the ashtrays, the browning coffee mugs, Mr. Rooster Chicken was the prime mover, the phenomenon that fledged the Ronson's lives with a meaning that now seemed inexplicable. A rakish chicken, looking back at the two men with dry eyes.

"You should get rid of all of this stuff," said Ethan.

Hank sighed and gave a rueful snort. "You're right. I probably should. Do you want another drink?"

"No thanks," said Ethan, "I should be making a move. Getting on. I've got to teach later."

Hank suddenly stirred himself like a host, setting his glass down, his hands moving with the business of seeing a guest off. "You should take something," said Hank. "I have to get rid of it. I should get rid of it all. Like you said. Why not start now. Take something."

"No," said Ethan. "It's all you."

"I insist," said Hank. "By way of thanks for covering my classes. And for talking. I do feel better."

"Well, if you insist." Ethan scanned the room, sweeping his head back and forth in the manner of a child who is pretending not to notice where the treat is hidden. He looked briefly at the ceiling. His eyes settled on the nesting doll, still on the coffee table. "Okay," he said, casually. "How about this?"

"Ahh," said Hank, hesitating. "Not that."

"Why not?"

"I like it. It's from Alina."

"Sure," said Ethan, shrugging. "It was just . . . right there."

"Yeah. How about the candlestick holders? From the dining room," said Hank, motioning to them, and then walking hurriedly in the direction he pointed. "They're Reed & Barton. Not cheap. Worth a lot, I think. Not that it matters." Hank removed the unused red tapers from a pair of white porcelain chicken figurines and set them aside on the table. He picked up each figurine in turn, running his thumb around their sockets to remove any crumb of wax. "I can wrap these in paper for you," he said, moving into the kitchen. "I should wrap these. Let me do that."

"Sure," said Ethan, moving up the steps toward the door. He noticed the folder for Hank's classes and tucked it under his arm. "Those are nice. Reed & Barton? I'll sell them on eBay. Good for you. Your first step. Moving on. We'll split the proceeds."

Hank stopped short, a sheet of newspaper in one hand ready to wad around a candleholder in the other. "No," he said. "You shouldn't . . . I mean, no, these are a gift. From me. You shouldn't sell them. Okay?" Hank stared at Ethan, his mouth drawn and strange.

"Okay," said Ethan simply, placating. A hint of the mournful tone returned. "I won't sell them. They'll look nice on our table. We'll use them for special occasions. Thank you."

Hank broke off his gaze and wrapped the figurines with a loud flourish of crinkling newsprint. "It's just that . . . ," he continued when he was done, "well, just promise me you won't sell them. Maybe just now I don't like the idea of people parting with things so easily. Anyway, they're a gift, from me. For you and Miriam. I don't remember if we even got you a wedding present. So take these, I want you to have them."

"Of course," said Ethan, reaching his hands to take the two twisted bundles of gray paper, feeling the smudge of ink catch against his fingers. "Thank you. Miriam will love them."

"Okay, then," said Hank. "Thanks again for covering my classes. I feel better. I really do."

"Yes," said Ethan, "of course, your classes. It'll be fine. You know. Just keep me posted."

Ethan stepped out onto the porch and waved briefly, holding both bundles in the crook of his left arm as Hank shut the door on the darkness inside. Ethan turned and exhaled and paused a moment on the stoop to let fresh air fill his lungs. Then he walked down the black asphalt driveway to his car.

The front windows of Ethan's Subaru wagon were rolled down. The back of the wagon was cluttered with the detritus of his domestic life with Miriam: a deflated Pilates ball, an empty water jug, a torn shopping bag of Goodwill books. Ethan leaned in through the passenger window and set the bundles of newsprint down on the seat before moving to the other side and settling in behind the steering wheel. Ethan lit a longed-for cigarette as he drove slowly out of the Ronson's cul-de-sac. He held his cigarette in the fingers of his right hand as he bumped the turn signal and looked to the left, waiting for a space to merge into the busy road home to Miriam. Beside him, as he turned, the nestled candleholders jostled, fragile and white, shining in the unfurling paper—eggs waiting to hatch.

a beginner's guide to leaving your hometown

IT WAS SEPTEMBER, THE END OF TOURIST SEASON. The throngs that clogged the sidewalks downtown were gone. The Grayline tour buses that crawled along the streets were gone. The T-shirt shops clustered near the docks on Franklin Street had closed hours after the last cruise ship headed south out of Gastineau Channel, down the Inside Passage. The sky, split summer long by the whine of floatplanes sightseeing along the coast or over the ice fields, was silent. Juneau was empty, ours again. It was in the midst of all this leaving that Wade again announced his firm intention to leave too.

Wade had lived with us, me and Tillie, for a month already, ever since his last girlfriend threw him out. We had a cramped apartment in a house at the top of Starr Hill, backed into the steep forested base of Mount Roberts. The house was owned by Butch Gardner, the man I crewed for, who lived upstairs with his family. Wade slept on the couch, his two duffle bags open and spilling into the living room. A nest of clothes, scattered empty notebooks, a foul-smelling sleeping bag. He had worked most of the summer at the Red Cedar, a fancy restaurant that opened and closed on the same schedule as the T-shirt shops. He stayed with us to conserve the little money he'd saved. Juneau rents are expensive; a place of his own would have cost him everything he had.

Tillie was four months pregnant and had every reason to complain, but she didn't. Wade had been my friend, off and on, since grade school, and she knew the affection I still had for him, as difficult as he could be. She accepted him into our apartment, she was kind to him in the way she would be kind to a dog, even when it tracked mud into the house, or left dishes in the sink, or watched movies stoned until 3:00 a.m. We weren't surprised when Wade said that he was buying a ferry ticket. Like most everyone we grew up with, he'd talked about leaving Juneau for years.

Wade made walk-on reservations on the *Columbia*, southbound on Tuesday mornings to Bellingham. A three-day trip: Sitka, Petersburg, Wrangell, Ketchikan, then Washington on Friday. Wade planned to find work in Seattle, or Portland maybe. He wanted to live someplace cheap, where he could write the novel he always talked about writing. "I can't do it here," said Wade. "Not with everyone in town breathing down my neck."

On his last day in town, Wade did laundry and tried to organize his mess into the duffle bags. I went down to the harbor to scrub out the *Kittiwake*, Butch's troller. It had been a lousy salmon season, prices in the toilet. We could have fished through September, gone after the late reds, but the keel was rotting out and Butch wanted to get it up on the dry dock before we went for halibut. The break suited me fine. I preferred being around with Tillie pregnant.

By early afternoon the lowering clouds started to drizzle. Nothing heavy. The sort of weather that generally passed for a nice day. Coming home, I saw Wade sitting on the porch, fidgeting and bored. He stood at my approach, flicking his cigarette into the narrow street. Tillie was at her mother's, he said. He'd finished packing, he called a few other friends to see if anyone wanted to get together, but no one called back. Wade was my height, about six foot. That was the only feature we shared in common. I had been a fat kid and he was skinny, but through the years we slowly traded places. Now, in our mid-twenties, he'd grown heavy while I could squeeze beneath a shut door. He wore his blond hair shaggy, and it suited him. Tillie's mom worked as a hair-dresser at the Nugget Mall and insisted on giving me a regular trim, lest I look like the shiftless fisherman she feared I was. But the main difference between us was that I tended to keep quiet, "your expres-sionless hatchet face," Tillie called it, while Wade broadcast everything he thought or felt. Now I could tell that he felt neglected, resentful, as though the town should have paused in his honor, to mark the imminent departure of a native son.

"Well, what do you want to do?" I asked.

"I don't know," said Wade. "Let's go somewhere. Go for a drive out the road or something."

"The glacier?" I suggested. "Who knows when you'll see it again."

"How about never." Wade lit another cigarette, exhaled a stream of smoke, and coughed. "What the hell. Sure, let's go to the glacier."

The passenger door of my rusted-out Datsun truck was perma-nently stuck, so Wade pushed in first. We drove down from Starr Hill, following Sixth Street to where it flattened out behind our old elementary school, and then we turned left and coasted down Main Street toward the water. The town of Juneau is tucked into the crotch of two mountains that plunge directly into the sea. Most of downtown is built up into the flanks of Mount Roberts and Mount Juneau. The business district, such as it is, is built on a narrow bench of flat land made from the fill of old mine tailings. At the edge is Gastineau Channel, a slice of the Pacific that cuts between Juneau and Douglas Island. There was little forethought given to the town's founding, threatened equally as it is by avalanche and tsunami, plagued by grim weather and endless damp, but it was where Joe Juneau had struck gold in 1880, and white people had lived there ever since, whether it was a good idea or not.

At the bottom of Main Street we turned right onto the long road, Egan Drive, and headed away from town. Egan follows the shoreline for thirty miles north before the pavement stops and goes to gravel. A mile after that the road dead ends. The road dead ends south of town, too. As does Douglas Highway. It's not a town you can depart casually. When you can get to a place only by boat or plane, you have to pay to leave.

Wade slouched as I drove, his head turned away, thinking about the past, or the future, I couldn't tell. Eight miles north of town the ridgeline of mountains fencing the coast breaks and a deep glacial valley cuts back some distance east. Mendenhall Glacier's long retreat had left ample space for cul-de-sac ranch homes, shopping malls, a Costco, a Wal-Mart, car dealerships. A bland helping of Everywhere America in the wilderness.

When we passed McDonald's Wade shifted upright and looked at me. "Do you remember, Silas? When the McDonald's came and we camped in the parking lot, waiting for it to open?"

I nodded. I remembered sleeping in the musty camper that Wade's dad usually parked on their lawn. Excited to be among the first to taste the freedom of Down South. Waking up groggy and waiting in line when the doors opened and not knowing what to order.

"What idiots we were," said Wade. "Thinking it was special."

"I remember," I said. "I thought it was good."

"You would, Silas."

At the next intersection we eased right, onto Mendenhall Loop. We passed through several miles of housing developments and boxy evangelical churches, until all buildings stopped abruptly as the road crossed into Tongass National Forest. Driving to the glacier is a form of time travel. The thick, old-growth forests of spruce and hemlock slowly give way to mixed stands of alder and willow, which dwindle to thickets of salmonberry and fireweed. The different plants signifying the length of time since the glacier uncovered the earth. At the face of the glacier, in the distance across Mendenhall Lake, nothing grows at all. Just scoured rock and melting ice. We pulled into the parking lot and sat in the truck for a moment, engine ticking.

"Figures," said Wade. "You can't get away from it."

We had expected the lot to be empty, but it was half full of cars and a press of people stood watching something in the lake below. When we got out of the truck, Wade scooting across the seat, we were pulled toward the crowd.

It was a mix of people, some I recognized, some not. Wade and I noticed Mr. Brock at the same time and Wade muttered under his breath. Mr. Brock had been our sophomore English teacher. He was retired now, but whenever he saw Wade he hassled him about going to college, told him he had such potential. He never noticed me. We skirted to the opposite edge of the crowd and looked out over the lake.

There was another group of people, fifteen or so, milling around just back from the rocky shore. There were folding chairs and stacks of equipment and tall reflective panels on tripods. Everyone's attention focused on a man with curly blond hair dressed in rugged buckskin leathers, trying to get into a kayak and making a hash of it. The kayak was afloat with an assistant to his knees in the water holding it steady. The buckskin man stood straight up in the cockpit, trying to balance as he sat awkwardly down. The boat tipped and the man kicked a leg out into the water up to his hip as the kayak swept away from him like a compass needle, spreading his legs. We could hear him cursing from where we stood. There was scattered laughter and some advice shouted from the crowd of locals. The man slogged to shore while the assistant dragged the kayak back on the beach.

"It's that magazine guy," said Wade. "A fucking cigarette ad. Unbelievable."

They toweled the buckskin man off, wiping down his legs. He ignored the crowd, while the director of the enterprise turned back and glared at us. "Could we have some quiet, please?" he yelled over his shoulder, his voice high and frustrated.

"Welcome to flavor country, bitches," said Wade. He decided he liked the phrase so he repeated it, shouting it back to the director, and laughed. Wade's laugh was distinctive—an explosive series of deep barks fringed with high pitches, like a circus sea lion. Once you heard it you always knew who it came from. I noticed Mr. Brock looking over at us with a disappointed expression, and I looked away quickly. Wade didn't mind a ruckus, but it made me uncomfortable.

Wade leaned into me. "See this? Alaska sells an image of itself, and they sell it back to us to sell cigarettes so we smoke and die. This place is going to kill me."

I nodded. "Maybe you should quit smoking."

The face of the glacier loomed across the lake, behind the buckskin man. A thick and dirty river of ice pulling back into the mountains from where it had come. Pulling back slowly and deliberately, like the antenna of a slug. Uncovering rock and soil that time hadn't touched for thousands of years. Places where no one had walked. Places that hadn't become anything yet. Where life started over.

Chunks of blue-and-white ice floated on the lake and the buckskin man, after he had been relaunched, paddled unsteadily toward them. He rested a moment and then lit a cigarette, letting it dangle from the side of his mouth.

In the middle distance a gravel bar fingered out into the lake from the alder thickets. I saw a dark shape skulking hesitatingly along it. Curious and halting. Others saw it too, and a mumble passed through our crowd, people pointing. The director noticed and turned to yell at us again. "Can one of you people get your dog out of the shot?" The buckskin man craned back to look and nearly lost his paddle.

"That's a wolf," someone shouted at him. "It's a black wolf."

The director studied the wolf for a moment. "Get it in the shot," he called out sharply. "Sandy, you might have to move." The man in the kayak pitched his cigarette in the lake and struggled to turn the boat. The wolf became skittish with the yelling. He froze stiff and bristling. After a pause, the wolf turned and cocked his leg, pissing briefly on a scrubby willow growing on the sandbar, and trotted back into the thicket along shore.

Wade barked his sea-lion laugh, coughing, leaning on my shoulder. The fitful drizzle that had waffled all day made up its mind and rained in earnest. The people in the photo crew hurriedly pulled on the thin rain ponchos the tourists wore, like dry-cleaner bags.

"C'mon, Wade," I said, moving away from the crowd. "C'mon, let's get out of here."

Wade wiped his eyes, still grinning. "Yeah," he said. "Let's go get shitfaced."

We got into the truck and drove downtown, retracing our steps. Like anyplace else, you drive it often enough and you don't notice it anymore. I could drive it in my sleep. With my eyes closed. In my dreams. Nothing but the regular thump of the wipers and Wade talking.

"Fucking Mr. Brock," he said. "He always gives me that pained look. Always trying to boss me around with his disappointment."

"At least he didn't come over and remind you about your potential."

"My potential," Wade echoed. He lit a cigarette and cracked the window. "What does Brock know about potential? Never having had any himself. He showed me some of his poems once. Did I tell you?"

I nodded.

"All rhyming about eagles and ravens and finding your spirit self in the forest. Pathetic."

In Mr. Brock's class we had read *Hamlet* aloud over several class sessions. Wade read the part of Hamlet, the tortured prince, his voice loud and plummy, pronouncing words none of us knew how to pronounce. I read Fortinbras, and stumbled over every syllable. Mr. Brock loved it, nodding along with Wade, exclaiming over his favorite passages. The experience energized Wade somehow. He took himself more seriously, and we drifted apart. It hurt me at the time, his drifting away. I read *Hamlet* again and again, wondering what to make of it.

"He was just being nice," I said finally. "At least he took an interest."

"He can keep it. No wonder everyone wants to leave this place. How do they expect people to live with everyone shaking their heads all the damn time."

"Not everyone," I said.

"Most everyone. Like this is supposed to be a close-knit community. Spaghetti feeds when people get sick and all that. But this isn't a community. It's just one big goddamn committee, always watching." He ashed out the window but the flakes blew back into the cab. He brushed his shirt with the back of his hand. "I should have left two years ago. I'd be done with my novel by now. I can't live here, Silas. Can't work here." Wade looked away, out the window, mouth tight. "I could be bounded in a nutshell," he whispered to himself, "were it not that I have bad dreams."

I knew about Wade's novel. He'd talked about it enough. It was about a man, a lot like Wade, in a town a lot like Juneau, who dates a sixteen-year-old girl from the Valley when he is twenty-two. The girl's father has him charged with statutory rape, and he spends three months in jail. After that the plot varies, but the basics of it stay the same. Wade and I were out of touch long before he dated Jessica, but I heard about it. Tillie found his mugshot on the sex offender registry. I didn't want to see but looked anyway. Wade's face was puffy, pale, and startled. I could tell he'd been crying, which surprised me. I'd been the crybaby when we were kids. Soon after seeing the picture, I went out to Lemon Creek to visit him.

Wade was sensitive about the whole thing, but no one else really cared. We all knew that he'd gotten a raw deal and we felt bad for him, or said we did anyway. Most everyone could relate one way or another. Butch had a DUI. Tillie had a minor consuming. Me and Wade had done plenty of lousy things—breaking windows, denting cars—when we were kids. But small-town forgiveness doesn't really work. Even as people forgive, they judge. I suppose I'm no different. I knew Wade felt the judgment, and there was no way to talk him out of feeling it.

Back downtown I parked on Front Street and we walked a block to the Imperial Bar. The town felt deserted after the crush of summer. It was five o'clock but already twilight. The sun was leaving us for winter too. The long bar of the Imperial was equally dead. Just regulars nursing cans of Rainier in the stale dimness. There was Sweaty Brian waving his hands as he talked to Shannon, the bartender. There was Remy the loudmouthed shrimper, who claimed to be the fleet highliner though I'd never seen him anywhere but hunched over his beer and shots of Hot Damn. Edwell, the owner, was standing on a barstool, taking down the crepe streamers and wilted balloons from the end-of-season party. Wade and I sat at the corner of the bar by the door and waited for Shannon to come over.

We sat there for hours, drinking. Time warped and split as it does. It stopped and started over in a new direction. Then another. The bar grew crowded and loud and smoky. The jukebox cranked on with the same songs that had played for years. With every person who came in, when the door banged shut, Wade turned to see if it was anyone he wanted to see or say good-bye to. None was. He ordered more and we drank more. A payphone hung on the wall, but I didn't call Tillie, who was asleep now anyway. Wade talked about Seattle, about Portland, about bands and jobs and his novel. He remembered the time we both got beat up after he sold a sandwich bag of oregano to a high schooler as pot. He talked about man's rule on earth and the darkness it brought. I nodded and waited for him to be done, knowing that it took a long time for Wade to be done.

"By god, Silas," Wade said, his voice emphatic, "we're standing on the shoulders of four million years of hominid evolution here. Those poor australopithecines, running around in Olduvai Gorge, getting eaten by lions. What are we going to say when we meet them someday, shake their hands? What have we done to justify their sacrifice? How have we advanced the ball? What have you done? Lived in Juneau and fished? Taken fish out of the water for people to eat and shit back into it? Christ, man." He swayed on his barstool and paused, raising his eyebrows in thought. "Not that there's anything wrong with commercial fishing. Honest work at least." He drained his pint. "But writing? I can advance the ball there. Be proud to shake Lacy's or what's-her-fuck's hand." He belched softly and stood, scraping the stool back on the scuffed linoleum floor and hitching up his pants. "I gotta piss."

The door banged shut and Wade turned. It was Liz, the girlfriend who kicked Wade out, and her new man, Scott, who worked at Fitness Plus. They strode by pointedly and went to the pool table in the back, hands on each other. Wade's mouth went sour. "I'm sick of this place," he said. "Let's get out of here."

I nodded. "I'll settle up." Wade went outside.

It took a while to find Shannon and pay. When I finally left, Wade was leaning next to the door, a plastic bag with a twelve pack of beer in it on the sidewalk. He was pissing on the side of the building, splattering his feet. "I got us beer at the Cache," he said. "Have one. Let's go to the docks."

"Jesus, Wade."

"Gotta piss somewhere," he said. "Not in there. Done with that. Besides, this is how I'll do it from now on. Like that wolf. Dogs don't piss in secret places. Not in bathrooms behind closed doors. No sir. They piss up high, so all who sniff know who is living up to their potential." He finished and took a beer from the crinkling bag, handing me one, leaning in close. "In fact," he said. "I'm not even zipping my fly. I have some marks to leave on this town."

He stared at me, his eyes intent and glassy. Waiting for me to make up my mind. I knew that look. Wade was my friend, and I knew what I was getting into. I shrugged. "It's your last night, man. Do it up."

So we walked the town, drinking beer from the shopping bag, stopping now and again for Wade to piss. He pissed in the doorway of the El Sombrero, where he had worked in high school. He pissed on the window of the Alaskan Hotel. He pissed on Nimbus, a large green abstract sculpture that used to be in the courthouse plaza but was now by the museum because some legislators from Anchorage hated it so much they passed a law mandating it be moved. He pissed on the flagpole in front of the State Office Building, and the one in front of the State Capitol. "How many flags do we have to fly to remind ourselves that we're part of America?" he asked.

It was late and cold and the walk took forever. Wade would go dry and then we'd sit and he'd drink another beer and he'd give me advice, until the urge came upon him again and we'd be off to the next spot, running down the street, shoes flapping. I went once, by the Arctic Bar on Franklin. I didn't feel bad about it; that stretch of sidewalk always smells like piss anyway.

The last stop was in front of the Marine View Building, where there is a sculpture of Joe Juneau. Wade staggered like he was wearing stilts on the deck of a pitching crabber, holding the last can of beer in his hand. "Here's to your town of gold," said Wade. "Gone gold-plated." He poured a slug of beer on the face of the founder and dropped the can on the sidewalk. It rolled to the curb, echoing along the empty street, and then stopped, held by a seam in the concrete. His head waggled loosely on his neck. "Let's go to the dock," he said. A dark stain appeared in his crotch.

"I think I'm done," I said. It was well after four in the morning. It was raining. "Let's go home."

"No. Gotta say good-bye."

I paused, decided not to fight it, and took his elbow, steering him in the right direction. He pulled his arm back sharply and grumbled, then put it close around my shoulders, leaning against me. We walked through Marine Park, past the band shell, to the wide-planked dock at the edge of Gastineau Channel. The rain came heavy now, and Wade sang in his doorbell voice, his breath hot and sour on my neck, "Neither snow nor rain, nor gloom of night, can stay these couriers . . . from their appointed rounds . . ."

On the dock he split away and spun a circle, arms wide and head back, tripping over his legs. Letting the rain fall on his face. I stood at the edge, arms crossed and cold, resting one foot up on the low wooden lip of the dock, thirty feet above the sea, looking across at Douglas Island. The tide was in full, sighing gently against the beach below. The fence of mountains hemmed all around us in the dark.

Yellow signs were posted along the edge of the dock, every fifty yards or so, marking the placement of straight steel ladders plunging down into the cold water of the channel. "Safety Ladder. Use at Your Own Risk." Wade read the offer aloud and laughed. "See, Silas?" he hooted, waving his arms at the sea, at the sky. "See? This is Alaska, right? Community? A safety ladder, use it at your own risk. Fuck Jack London and Robert Service. This is what it is. What it is now. If someone could *nail* that, could *write* that, that would be something wouldn't it?" He spun again and stumbled and laughed. "When I do that, it will be something."

It was getting near five now. I was wet. My head was hurting. "Well do it then," I said. "Just stop talking about it for once. How many goddamn empty notebooks do you need? You hate our hometown, fine. I get it. But I live here, and you know I love it. So just write what you want or get over it. This is getting old."

Wade stopped and straightened. "What?"

"I'm done," I said. "I just want to go home."

He looked at me, his protruding mouth silent and angry, his face twisted.

"C'mon, man," I said. "Let's just go home. I'm cold. You've pissed yourself. You must be cold too. What time is your ferry?"

Wade was still, his face blank. Then in a sudden movement he pulled his pants down, kicking off his shoes. He wadded up his pants and threw them over the edge of the dock. He pitched his shoes in too, letting the first splash before he threw the other, overhand, as far out into the darkness as he could. "Fuck you," he said, standing in his soiled white underwear, trembling. "I don't have a home."

"You do," I said. "So do I. Let's go there."

He cursed me again and turned his back, walking away down the dock. "Where the hell am I supposed to go, Silas?" he wailed over his shoulder. "Where are you supposed to go when the last fucking frontier is ruined for you? Where else? What am I supposed to do, Silas?"

Wade stumbled away, waving his arms as he continued the conversation with himself. I left him there. Sometimes the only way to end a play is for the audience to leave. I tucked my hands into my jacket and walked home, up the steep incline of Starr Hill. The windows were dark, but Tillie had left the porch light on. I hung my wet coat outside and stepped into the stillness of our home.

I drank some water, showered to wash off the night, and slipped beneath the cool sheets next to Tillie. She smelled of lavender and warmth. She was lying on her side, facing the wall, sound asleep. I spooned up next to her and listened to her regular breath for a moment before I reached my hand over her stretched belly, feeling for our child, stirring in its darkness, untouched yet by time.

Some nights on the *Kittiwake*, when Butch wasn't snoring, I could hear the whales singing through the hull. Their trills and moans and growls and chirps. Singing as they swam, their song echoing through the water, echoing in the nighttime. I held my hand over Tillie's belly, thinking of the whales and our own fishy creature. Tillie stirred and murmured, wrapping her arm tightly around mine, pinning me to her.

Around dawn the front door shuddered open and then closed again softly. I lay awake for a while before pushing free of the bed. Wade was curled on the floor, knees to his chest, arms around his head. His naked legs were mottled blue with cold. I heaved him onto the couch and covered him with a blanket, tucking it under his chin, under his gaping mouth, the scent of his breath like the stale water in a vase of cut flowers.

Later in the morning, Tillie and I would cook breakfast. We had frozen sausage links and some eggs. I'd add oregano to them and Wade would laugh about the time we got beat up in the graveyard. Then we'd all walk downtown, and when the tide went out Wade and I would look for his pants and shoes under the cruise ship docks. We'd find them, between the barnacled rocks strewn with kelp and sea lettuce. Eventually the tide would come back in, wiping the slate clean, starting over again. And in due time, Wade would once more announce his firm intention to leave Juneau for good.

sleight

MY FATHER WAS A MAGICIAN. He could pull a penny from your ear, pick your card, or make things disappear. Once, he made my mother disappear for three months. My little brother, Joker, and I hunted for her everywhere: the guest bedroom, the garden shed, the garage, even so far as the third step from the bottom in the dank and dripping basement. We pleaded to be let in on the gag. My father said Mother's apparent disappearance was a singular illusion and that a true magician never revealed his secrets.

Mother was gone for an entire summer. That July, I turned nine. While Joker and I sat on the crabgrass in the shadow of the garden shed, Father performed a birthday magic routine. He pulled pennies from our ears, picked our cards, and made Joker's disintegrating stuffed elephant disappear. We were a restive audience. Our teeth ached from the red-sugared icing of the grocery-store sheet cake. Mosquitoes bit our scalps. We failed to express our delight. "Old hat," we cried. "We are not impressed."

The apparent disappearance of Elephant alarmed Joker. He studied Father as our old man fussed with his tuxedo jacket and arranged the red-checked tablecloth and pointed at a jet plane passing beyond hearing overhead. Father squinted into the sun and the beads of sweat on his reddening forehead glistened. "A contrail is like chalk on a chalkboard, isn't it boys? Amazing how it flies."

"Where's Elephant?" asked Joker.

"Everyone wants to fly away, don't they boys?" Father dabbed his forehead. He nudged a small cardboard box beneath the warped folding table with a sandaled foot. He twitched the red-checkered cloth.

"Where's Elephant?" repeated Joker.

Father grinned. "A singular illusion." He opened his hands and a gray dove burst forth in a flurry of noise and feathers that propelled the bird a descending twelve feet before it hit the fence and pitched open-winged and panting on a dirt patch.

"Dehydrated," observed Father.

"Where's Elephant," demanded Joker.

I asked, "Where's Mom?"

Pulling a penny from a child's ear requires sleight of hand. Step one is the right-handed display of the coin. In step one it is vital to spark excitement about the penny. The magician could say, for instance, "Here is the true copper, boys, pressed by the United States Mint in 1983. Abraham Lincoln!" The patter is key because everyone knows that a penny is worthless, whether it comes from your ear or not.

Step two is tucking the penny between the puffy flesh at the inside base of your ring and middle fingers, as though the space was a coin slot on a payphone and you wanted to call someone faraway but all you had was a penny. Display your hands: the penny is gone, as though eaten by a machine that doesn't take pennies but also doesn't give them back.

Step three is distraction. Call your audience's attention to the crusted dishes in the sink, or the piles of moldering clothes in the living room. Say: "Things sure are falling apart around here, aren't they, boys?" Your audience's eyes will cloud over as they imagine flying far away, leaving nothing behind but a fading chalk line. Transfer the penny to the coin slot on your left hand.

Step four is the finale. The penny is in your left hand now, warm between your fingers. Notice that an audience member's ears are dirty. "Carrots could grow in there," you say. Feign surprise and concern. Suggest that a carrot is growing now, at this very moment, its green fronds emerging from your audience member's dirty ear. As you theatrically extend your trembling left hand toward the ear, use your thumb to retrieve the penny and pinch it solid between your thumb and index finger. Then say, "My stars! Look what I found." If the audience member fails to express delight, say: "Abraham Lincoln!"

Even after the return of Elephant, my little brother remained alarmed. Joker took to Mother's closet and refused to come out. He built a fort beneath Mother's hanging dresses and behind her jumble of shoes. He tucked his knees to his chest and pulled his racecar T-shirt over them. He withdrew his arms and face into the T-shirt tent, leaving only a bedhead feather of black hair waving above the collar. My brother became a barnacle on the bottom of the ocean, a crustacean clinging to the dusty floor of the Mother-scented sea. He swam to shore only when no one was around. From the kitchen, Father and I would occasionally hear the pipe-rumbling flush of the upstairs toilet.

"The thing with barnacles," explained Father, as he made sandwiches, "is that they lack a sense of adventure."

"You also once said," I countered, "that if you stay put in one place long enough, you'll see the entire world."

Father paused, with the knife deep in the peanut butter, and cast his eyes about our disintegrating home. "Well, Ace," he said, "we're sure as shit seeing something now, aren't we?" He gave me the knife to lick clean. "After lunch," he said, "maybe you should wash your ears."

For my ninth birthday I received a copper-colored Huffy bicycle to which I gave a secret name. I pedaled furiously and developed my sense of adventure. The streets around our home were named for coins and cards: Jefferson, Queen, Washington, King, Eisenhower. I pedaled in the rain and thereby cleansed my ears. I entered the vacant houses of vacationing neighbors and smelled their closets. None carried the scent of the sea. I stole from their coin dishes, but none of their pennies brought me luck.

Some of the pilfered money went to the feeding and rehabilitation of Father's panting dove. Barbary doves, also known as ringneck doves, or white doves, or *Streptopelia risoria*, are easily trained to suffer handling. Slipped into a tuxedo sleeve, they will remain hidden, heart thumping and warm, until needed. They are not burdened by alarm. First they are in one place, and then they are in another; this they placidly accept as the natural course of events. Doves, when healthy, are not suited to magic shows in outdoor venues. Unlike pigeons, they lack a homing instinct. Once on the wing, doves do not return.

School and Mother both returned in September. Mr. Anthony cursived his name on our fourth-grade chalkboard and the contrails remained even after he erased it for fractions. Mother seemed erased for the duration of the single week she stayed. Faint and thin, barely visible. She kept to her bed.

"Dehydrated," observed Father.

Joker sniffed her sleeping neck and returned to the closet.

"Where has she been?" I asked.

"Adventuring," said Father.

Picking a card requires memory. Hold the deck of cards in your left hand in the dealer's position and then spread the top of the deck into your right hand, creating a fan between the halves. Invite an audience member to choose a single card. Tell her to examine the card closely and commit it to memory. Tell her that fate has delivered her this card; that it belongs to her out of all possible cards. While the audience member absorbs the singular injustice of this information, peek at the card as though it was a page from her private diary. Return it to the deck. Later, when you confront her with the card, do not be surprised if she bursts into tears and flees from the venue.

There is no magic to making things disappear. Given time and inattention, the world tends toward absence. Stuffed elephants disintegrate, pennies slip between cushions, contrails fade. Doves released do not return. My father the magician, aged and bewildered with dementia, announced that the disappearance of his mind was his greatest trick. Joker and I, by then both paunchy and distracted, magicians ourselves, sat as our old man twitched the bedclothes and tried to remember his card. "You know, boys," he said, "the singular illusion is that any of it seemed to exist at all." There was an uneasy pause. Joker and I were restive. We failed to express delight. So Father said: "Abraham Lincoln!"

knots pull against themselves

WHEN MARTY SNEEZED, JAKE DIDN'T SAY ANYTHING. Not a word, not even a nod of the head. That was him in a nutshell. A polite person, a tractable person, they'd say bless you. For the soul's protection, or politeness at least. But not Jake. He was impolite and cussed about it. Marty strained to remember whether Jake had ever said it, god bless or gesundheit or anything, when they were kids. He couldn't recall one way or another. Hard to believe that they were brothers, being so different. Marty noticed a few wet spots shining on the dashboard of Jake's truck. Jake was driving, eyes focused ahead, smoking a cigarette. He hadn't seen. Marty sniffled and settled back into the bench seat.

"I need to get some gas," said Jake. "You're paying."

"It's your truck."

"I'm doing you a favor. You asked. You're paying."

"I could have taken a taxi," said Marty.

"And you would've had to pay for that too."

"At least it would have been on time."

They were on Douglas Highway just before the bridge. It was already seven thirty in the morning and the flight south to Seattle left at 8:40. Driving to the airport normally took twenty minutes, so it was all right that Jake showed up later than Marty asked. The two weren't close; they rarely even talked. But Marty refused to ask Mother for a ride, and he didn't want to pay for a cab. And perhaps he wanted someone to say good-bye to. Marty knew he should be grateful that Jake showed up at all.

Marty turned to glimpse through the flat rear window of the truck, checking on his suitcase in the back. It was still there. Of course it was. All the same he felt the need to check. The suitcase seemed dry, even with the steady drizzle falling. They slowed at the bottleneck merge where cars from North Douglas and South Douglas vied to cross the two-lane bridge into Juneau. Marty sighed at the line of cars and pushed a hand into his jacket pocket, feeling for his plane ticket. Just checking.

"Plenty of time," said Jake. He exhaled a stream of smoke through the brush of his moustache. "And wipe that shit off my dashboard."

Marty ignored him, as though he hadn't heard and then leaned forward and quickly swiped the dashboard with the sleeve of his jacket. When he sat back he noticed a smear of thick grime on his sleeve. A yellowish brown stain, a mix of grease and dust, the precipitate of the stale tobacco fug thickening the air. Disgusting. Marty brushed at his sleeve and cracked the window. With the window open, the rattle and shake of Jake's truck grew louder. Laughable to care about some spit on the dash with the truck itself falling apart. The truck seemed to collect bad luck: rusting dents, a missing bumper, a cracked windshield, a busted taillight. All sad stories.

The traffic eased forward slowly, and the tempo of the truck's rattle amplified as they started up the incline of the bridge. It was late August. Already it felt like fall. Marty looked to his right, south down Gastineau Channel. A low haze of gray clouds obscured the mountains and the Juneau waterfront. A troller emerged from beneath the bridge, stabilizer poles erect and a curling wake behind. In the distance Marty could see a late-season cruise ship, festooned with paling lights. The ship, like a recumbent skyscraper, dwarfed any building in town. In middle school Marty's class toured one of the new galaxy-class ships on a field trip. Even then he knew it was public relations for the cruise line, an attempt to mollify the locals who grumbled at the rain-ponchoed tourists. But once inside the ship Marty forgot about that. It was so clean and sparkling and enchantingly fine. It had chandeliers and wide burgundy-carpeted corridors. The passengers appeared crisply dressed and sophisticated, laughing and speaking long sentences in well-accented conversation. No one wore sweatpants or mumbled or smelled of mildew and cheap wine. It was elegant, like a picture-book castle, and his yearning to stay struck him like a pain. When the class made its way down the gangway back to the dog shit–spotted dock, Marty eyed the mooring ropes, thick as his twelve-year-old thigh, and imagined for a moment shimmying aboard as a stowaway. He would be caught, of course, but quickly identified as a brilliant and charming personage, welcome to travel to all the world's glittering ports. He noticed then the large metal disk clamped midway along each taut rope—shields against rats—and knew that he could not hazard it. As he stepped aboard the idling school bus, with its corrugated floor and green vinyl benches and scent of damp feet, he decided to leave Juneau as soon as he could.

A green light allowed Jake to pass across Egan Drive and turn into the Tesoro station for gas. He pitched his cigarette before they pulled to a stop next to a dirty pump. He cut off the engine and the truck dieseled briefly then went quiet. Jake held out his hand to Marty.

"Give me ten bucks, but put in nine. I need a coffee."

Marty reached for his wallet and reluctantly pulled a five and four ones.

"Buy your own. I need this."

Jake grinned at him. "A cab'd cost you twenty."

Marty dug back in his wallet for another dollar. "A cab would already be dropping me off."

"You worry too much," said Jake as he slid from the bench and slammed the door. Marty watched Jake's thin body stride at an angle toward the brightly lit station. Jake walked with his head cocked to one side, tacking to his destination, never coming straight on. He pulled open the door and strode back to the bathrooms, his crewcut bobbing above the shelves of chips and Hostess cakes. Marty pushed out and went around the tailgate of the truck to the pump. When the gas was clicking in, he rested his elbows on the truck's gunnels. Most of the truck bed was cluttered with the tools of Jake's painting business: a sprayer, buckets, splattered tarps, a short extension ladder. Marty shook out a tarp and covered his suitcase against the rain. Everything he needed for his new life was packed inside. A pocket bulged with the clothes he planned to change into when he reached Seattle: a clean white button-down shirt, rep tie, and an argyle sweater. What he imagined to be East Coast Collegiate. His life would begin in three hours. A layover in Seattle, then Detroit, then Bangor. He checked his watch. It was a quarter to eight. Marty startled. Lulled by the steady click of the pump, he had forgotten the flowing gas. He released the handle just as the price rolled to fourteen dollars.

"Hey moneybags," shouted Jake, leaning out of the station door, "get your ass over here." He flung his arm in a sweeping gesture, beckoning. "I said nine bucks. Dammit. Now I'm short."

Marty hustled across. The station was empty but for a Tlingit woman behind the counter eyeing them both with a noncommittal smile. Marty opened his wallet. "How much?" he asked.

"And a coffee," said Jake, filling a cup from the sputtering airpot. He pressed down on the black disk and the pot gave out, spewing droplets and fumes. "Hey," said Jake to the woman, "this one's empty."

The woman left her place behind the counter and refilled the airpot from a diner-style glass decanter that had been warming on a hotplate. The woman was maybe twenty, with a willowy girlish frame and dark eyes. She wore white stirrup stretch pants and a long blue sweater and tucked her long black hair behind her ears as she moved deliberately through her actions. Jake followed her with his eyes, a sly look on his face. Marty checked his watch impatiently. "Can't you just pour it into to the cup?" he asked. He looked at Jake. "Can't you just . . . ?" He motioned as though he was holding a cup to the decanter. "C'mon."

Jake grinned at him and then turned to the woman, who was back behind the counter, below the upside-down shelves of cigarettes. "This is my little brother," said Jake, winking. "He thinks he's King

Shit of Fuck Mountain because he has a plane to catch to go to college. He's in a hurry."

The woman stared back at Jake and then glanced at Marty. She shrugged, never losing her smile, and rang up the gas and coffee. "Fifteen dollars nine cents," she said.

Marty grimaced. He wanted to say to her and Jake, to shout, "Colby. Colby College. In Maine. Do you know how hard it is to get admitted there? Do you know what that means? You idiots." But he did not. He added five and a quarter to Jake's outstretched ten and waited for the change. Jake lingered at the counter, fitting a black plastic lid on his cup of coffee. He blew across the puckered hole to cool it and drank. Marty bit his tongue.

Jake squinted through the smoke of another cigarette as he merged back onto Egan Drive, heading north. The truck rattled and Jake coughed. That was fitting. Jake and the truck were two of kind: both battered and gasping. All sad stories. Jake was just six years older than Marty, but he looked forty. His thin face was pitted and pale, his moustache flecked with gray. Even at fifteen Jake had a moustache. Sparser than the one he sported now but a moustache all the same. Marty had envied it fiercely. Envied, in fact, most everything about Jake—his freedom, his stiff black leather jacket that creaked when he bent his arms, his ability to tell their mother to shove it. Marty attempted once to adopt his brother's tone with Mother and got slapped. "Don't you start all that shit too," Mother said, before pulling Marty tight to her, squeezing him into her breasts. She inhaled deeply, which bound them even closer, and then she sighed, signaling the start of a crying jag. "Don't you start, too." Soon after that Jake started getting arrested and Marty recoiled from his example. Mother said Jake was a lost cause. "You're the only man of this house," she told Marty. "It's just you and me."

"She was hot," said Jake, exhaling a plume of smoke. "I should get gas there more often. Don't have any Tlingit girls in Maine. Think of everything you're gonna be missing."

"Whatever."

"I mean really, Colby? That's a cheese. What is it, a cooking school?"

"You don't understand anything about it."

Jake snorted. "Right," he said.

The snort was Jake's response to most everything. It was his stock answer whenever he got in trouble. His first arrests were the usual things for a fifteen-year-old with a leather jacket in a small town: tickets for cigarettes, joyriding, minor consuming. Jake seemed proud of it. Proud of the late night calls and Mother having to go to the police station to collect him. She hassled him about paying her back for the fines, about doing his service hours, but he would smirk and snort and say it was no big deal, and she threw up her hands. She unburdened herself to Marty, soliciting an adult sympathy, which he found satisfying to give. Once Jake came home stinking of pot and Mother sought out Marty's eyes for a knowing look. Marty lifted an eyebrow as if to say, what can you do? Jake glared and shut himself up in the room he shared with Marty, locking them out for the rest of the night. On such occasions Marty slept on the couch in the cluttered main room, or slept with Mother. He didn't mind. They became a team, Marty and Mother, two ropes tied with a knot so firm that Jake, with his bitten fingernails, could not undo it.

As they picked up speed on Egan, the drizzle turned to a heavy rain, and Jake switched the wipers to a higher speed. They passed the boat harbor and Juneau-Douglas High School and the Breakwater Hotel, following the shoreline of the channel. The two southbound lanes, separated from the two northbound by a wide grass median, were clogged with state workers heading into the downtown office buildings. Marty didn't feel in the least nostalgic as they pulled away from downtown. He was glad to pass these places and put them behind.

Jake was pointing out houses as they drove. Big houses built up into the flanks of Mount Juneau, overlooking the channel. "See that one?" said Jake. "I had that job but couldn't get to it." He pointed to another. "Had that one under contract and the fucker backed out when I couldn't give him a completion date. It's the weather. Rains too goddamn much. Can't paint when it rains. I should sue him." He pointed to a few more without speaking. Then he said, "I know all the houses in this town." Marty raised his eyebrows at that, almost an involuntary action. As though he was still looking across the room at Mother, saying what can you do?

The summer Jake turned sixteen the police arrested him for a series of burglaries. Houses all over town, they said. Mother let the cops in and did nothing as they took Jake except to say that she didn't want to be bothered about it. "You can be there when we interview him," said one of the cops. His bristling moustache put Jake's to shame. "It's your right, as a parent." Mother shook her head and said that it was no big deal. Later that night Marty and Mother watched a movie comedy on video. Mother melted butter and made popcorn and they ate it together from a large bowl, laughing, their fingers coated in grease.

Marty checked his watch. Two minutes after eight. He watched the road ahead, the Yacht Club passed slowly on their left. Jake was leaning forward over the steering wheel, craning his neck to look up at the houses on the hillside as though checking their paint. Marty eyed the speedometer. The needle lazed at forty-five miles per hour. "C'mon man," said Marty finally, the irritation pitching his voice high and whiny. "Can't we go any faster? It's like you want me to miss my plane."

Jake kept the speed steady, the hint of a smile playing on his face. "I don't want you to miss your plane. I'm happy for you and all that. But if I go much faster we're liable to blow a rod."

Marty's irritation moved quickly into unease and then to the beginnings of panic. He was going to be late. He would miss his connections. He would have to pay and he could not afford to pay. His budget was exact to the dime until the loans came through and he did not know when the loans would come through. And he was already down fifteen dollars nine cents. He would be stuck and unable to leave. He would have to turn around and sleep in a childhood bed in a room that smelled of mildew, and he could not do that. He could not be stuck in this drowning town. He already felt nauseous from getting up so early. Now his face went hot and his eyes burned. "But I have to check a bag," he croaked.

"All right, all right," said Jake, pressing the accelerator down. The truck gained speed easily; the rattling even seemed to diminish. "Don't get your pussy broke. You'll make it in plenty of time."

Though Mother did not attend the police interview, they both went to Jake's arraignment. Jake wore green cotton prison scrubs and cheap plastic slippers. He looked grim and greasy and unwashed. His eyes and nostrils were red. The prosecutor read aloud the criminal complaint in a disinterested tone. He described how a woman came home one night to find Jake standing in her living room as though he was in a trance. She was a school aide and recognized him. He ran only after she yelled at him twice to get out. A man chased someone fitting Jake's description after finding him eating a bowl of cereal at his kitchen table, the door of the refrigerator still open. Around the same time there were other reports of houses entered and disturbed, doors left ajar, windows broken, belongings moved or taken. The prosecutor read a predictable list of stolen items: A stereo, a laptop, money. But the list also mentioned collectable thimbles, a large snow globe, bronzed baby shoes, a family snapshot in a silver frame, a Franklin Mint figurine of a golden retriever. When Marty met his eyes across the dingy courtroom, he thought Jake flinched. Two weeks later, when Jake plead out and took a deal for five months, he didn't look at Marty at all. During both hearings Mother dabbed at her face with a Kleenex and sniffled loudly and gripped Marty's hand tight. After the court officer led Jake away, Mother pulled Marty close. "Just you and me," she said.

The road was clicking by faster. They made the green light at the hospital intersection and passed Twin Lakes. The light at Vanderbilt Hill Road went red before they reached it. Jake slowed the truck to a stop and drummed his fingers on the steering wheel, whistling tunelessly. Marty struggled to breathe. He tried not to check his watch. The panic expanded in him. Like someone desperate for the bathroom, Marty could concentrate on only one thing at a time. His eyes focused straight ahead, staring with a blank intensity at the dashboard, the hood of the rattling truck. He did not look up at the fence of mountains looming above the fetid landfill to their right, or at the equally fetid alluvial mudflats to their left. He could think only of the plane. And why didn't he call a cab. And why didn't he break down and ask Mother for a ride. He had avoided both options because they were both expensive in their different ways. Marty and Mother had hardly spoken for seven months. Ever since he said that he was leaving, she had become peevish and resentful. As though he had done her an injury. He found the strained silence a relief. That morning, as he finally heard Jake's truck in the parking lot outside their apartment, he knocked on Mother's door and pushed it open.

Her room smelled of bad breath and box wine. "I'm leaving now," Marty said. She did not stir. He took his suitcase and rushed from the apartment to Jake's waiting truck as though escaping a caving mine shaft.

"How's Mom?" Jake had asked, after Marty stowed his suitcase and they were easing down the driveway.

Marty shook his head. "We don't get along," he said. "I'm glad to get out of here."

Jake wiped his mouth and lit a cigarette. "That's what you get for being loved," he said.

The parking lot was the closest to the apartment Marty had seen Jake in years. After being released from Cornerstone he dropped out of high school and lived with friends somewhere in the Valley. He came back once, knocking on Marty's bedroom window late at night, drunk and sopping wet from the pouring rain. Marty cracked the window and Jake said, "I just want to tell you, I didn't take any of the expensive things they said. I never took a computer. What would I do with it? I just wanted to see what other people lived like, you know? To be inside a nice house for a while and pretend. That's all." Jake looked blearily past Marty at the walls of the room they used to share. "You took down all my posters," he said simply. "I thought you liked those." Jake didn't notice the snow globe on the nightstand, or didn't mention it. After Jake left, tacking back into the darkness, Marty couldn't sleep. He shook the globe again and again, watching the snow settle and bounce on the diorama of a quaint, bucolic New England town. Marty had found the globe where Jake hid it in the back of their closet, stuffed inside a boot. He considered turning it in to the police, but chose not to. He sprayed the glass with Windex and wiped Jake's fingerprints away, making it his own.

In the truck it was 8:10 and they were at the Fred Meyer intersection, waiting to turn left across the southbound lanes onto Yandukin Drive, the road to the airport. Marty rocked in his seat, looking ahead at the stream of state workers heading into town. The cars were maddeningly spaced, each following the other just close enough to make turning dangerous. Marty's fingers were clenched white on his knees. He wanted Jake to defy the traffic, to gun the engine and pull out like a rabbit. He could not bear another second. "Go!" he yelled. Jake laughed and floored it, sending the truck squealing across the lane. Oncoming cars honked and braked and fishtailed as Jake sped onto Yandukin. Marty gave a terrified whoop and Jake cackled like an outlaw. With the adrenaline coursing through his body and blood echoing in his ears, Marty did not notice the lights of a police car behind them. Not until Jake began cursing and the truck slowed to a stop on the shoulder.

Marty's mind went blank. In the distance he could see the tailfin of a jet plane. The airport was a quarter mile from where they sat. The cop was out of his car, behind them writing in a notebook. Taking his time.

Jake watched the cop in the rearview mirror and snorted. "Fucking Vandiver," he said. He drummed his thumbs on the steering wheel and let out a long sigh.

Marty fumbled for the door handle. "I'll talk to him."

"No," said Jake. "He's a prick. I'll talk to him."

Jake waited until the cop approached the truck and then rolled down his window.

"Driving a little crazy back there weren't you?" said the cop, leaning down to look into the truck, at Marty.

Jake shrugged and mumbled something.

"Shut off the engine, please," said the cop. "I can't hear you clearly."

"We're in a hurry," said Jake.

"That's no excuse to drive like you did. You been drinking, Jake?"

"Nope. Get close and smell my breath if you want, Vandiver. I know you dig that sort of thing."

"What was that?" Vandiver clicked his tongue on his teeth, making a sharp sucking sound. He eyed Jake. "I thought I heard you say something." Vandiver reached out a hand. "Let's see your license."

"Christ, Vandiver, you know who I am. Can't you just write out the fucking ticket so we can get on?"

"Watch your tone, Jake Patchett. Kill your engine, close your mouth, and surrender your operator's license before we have a problem."

Jake snorted and turned to Marty, smirking. It was Jake's smirk saying can you believe this? Saying no big deal. But Marty's face was white and drained and sweating. His look was pleading. Don't let everything be ruined, Marty was repeating in his head. Don't let everything be ruined. Don't let this be fated to turn out wrong. I will be stuck forever in this black life. No ship. No road. Don't make me waste here in this small corner. Don't make me turn gray in these same houses. Please please please. Marty's chest shuddered and tears streamed from his eyes. His nose ran. Jake's smirk faded and his face went slack. He turned off the ignition and dropped his hands to his lap.

"Look, Officer Vandiver," he said quietly, his voice even and deflated, "I didn't mean any disrespect. I apologize. We're late for the airport and it's my fault. My little brother is going to college and he can't miss his plane. That's all."

Marty sniffled loudly and wiped his face with his hand. Vandiver leaned down to look through at Marty again. He stared at him for a moment, assessing him with his pale blue eyes. Finally he stood.

"That's your brother?" he asked Jake.

Jake nodded.

The cop clicked his tongue on his teeth and closed his notebook, tucking it away in his back pocket. "I'd rather you were leaving, Jake, but I'm sure we'll be seeing you around," he said. He rapped the roof of the truck with his knuckles twice. "Fix your taillight." Vandiver turned and walked back to his cruiser.

Jake exhaled slowly and restarted the truck. He pulled out a handkerchief and passed it to Marty without looking at him. He shifted the truck into drive and gravel sprayed as he pulled back up onto the road, eyes fixed ahead. Marty wiped his face with the handkerchief and held it clutched in his hand. Neither spoke.

In less than a minute they were at the small airport. Jake looped around the parking lot and pulled alongside the curb. Marty twisted in his seat, trying to see if there was a line at the check-in counter. "Okay," said Jake. Before the truck came to a full stop Marty was out and hoisting his suitcase from beneath the paint-splattered tarp. He turned and put a hand on the open door. "Be good," said Jake. "God bless and all that." Marty nodded and couldn't find any words and shut the truck door and hustled into the terminal. When he realized that he was still clutching the handkerchief, he looked back over his shoulder and saw that the truck was gone.

Marty arrived in Waterville after dark, so he didn't see the strip malls and shuttered buildings. He could believe for a time that it was all he'd hoped for. A place of elegance and lofty talk and roaring winter fires where he'd be invited to sing four-part harmony before tucking into a fine dinner. Where he'd be recognized as what he wanted to be, welcomed grandly, and guided to the world's glittering ports. Instead, as time wore on, he found himself feeling like a wharf rat who had mistakenly made it past the metal disk. A fraud. His roommate was a rich boy from Choate who dressed like an Alaskan fisherman, laughed at Marty's collection of argyle, and casually mentioned books that Marty was embarrassed to admit he hadn't even heard of. He found himself lying about everything. Telling fantastic stories that no one believed but no one challenged, for they were too polite to mock him to his face.

Marty wrote several letters to Jake, but they came back, returned all together, a month later. He put them in a box in his closet, below his jacket. The sleeve was still smeared with grime, even though Marty tried to wash it off. He remembered biting his tongue in the gas station, his moment of restraint, and was glad for the small relief it brought.

Before Christmas, he received a postcard from Mother saying that Jake was back in jail. Lemon Creek Correctional this time. She didn't mention for what. The picture on the postcard was of Juneau in summer: the mountains so high and the spruce forests so green and the channel so sparkling that no one would believe a place could be so beautiful unless they had seen the real thing and knew it to be true. Marty held the card a long while and then set it on his narrow desk, next to the snow globe he had carried with him, wrapped in clothes. He lifted the globe and shook it. He watched the Styrofoam pearls swirl and then fall, settling on the small drowning town it contained.

every island
longs for
the continent
kodiak, 1973

PHILIP LEKAS HEARD THE GROAN OF A DIESEL through the spruce trees—the sound of a truck struggling up the rutted driveway. Gravel crunched as the truck stopped next to the cabin and the driver cut the engine. Philip mustered his strength and lurched out of bed. He shuffled unsteadily to the narrow skylight facing out from the shingles of their small rented A-frame cabin. The side of the truck announced *Wagner Furniture* in fading gold letters. A heavily built man in brown coveralls stepped down from the driver's side and walked to the rear of the truck, popping the latch and sending the panel door roaring up on its rollers. A younger man jumped from the passenger side holding a pair of gloves in his hand. He wandered a few steps and twisted sharply to stretch his back. Philip caught a glimpse of his face as he turned. The young man had dark skin and black hair. An Aleut, he noted without interest.

Philip pushed away from the window and collapsed back into the gritty bed. Waves of fatigue pressed him into the mattress. A new sofa. He could hear Donna moving downstairs, her heels clacking as she rushed around. No one in Kodiak wore shoes inside, he had told her. She never listened. She wanted a new sofa to replace the ratty one on cement blocks that came furnished with the cabin. She wanted something nice, she had said, and the old sofa could stay in the shed until they moved out. He had protested that they couldn't afford anything nice just yet, and that he didn't want to clutter his studio. She gave him a slightly pitying look when he described the shed as his studio, but he thought she had understood about not being able to afford new furniture. Directly below him their infant, Nicholas, began to cry.

The heavy tread of boots sounded on the porch. The furniture men stomped off mud as they walked. Donna greeted them in a high friendly voice, talking over Nicholas's hiccoughing wail. Philip was reluctant to leave the thin, uncomfortable mattress. He felt too weak to go to work, too weak to call in sick even. But he couldn't miss his shift at the hospital now. Not if they had a sofa to pay for on top of everything else.

He heard the men return to the truck and start the engine to back it closer to the porch stairs. They slid out the metal ramp. There were the sounds of something heavy being moved: a scrape and a curse. The cabin shuddered and something fell massively on the porch. A cluster of notes, off-key but distinct, almost a minor seventh. A piano. Philip sat up.

Again he pushed away the bedclothes and stood. He wore only briefs, grayed from washing. His skin showed yellowish beneath the stubble on his gaunt face. Dark circles ringed his eyes. He grabbed Donna's bathrobe from the floor and tied its sash around his waist before making his unsteady way down the wooden steps from the A-frame's loft.

The two men were negotiating an upright piano through the front door. The large man pushed from the porch, grunting instructions at the young Aleut man standing inside. The young man grappled with the piano awkwardly, like a wrestler searching for purchase, straining to lift the piano to the angle necessary to ease it through the door. Donna stood a few feet away, watching. She wore a light green princess-line dress patterned with unlikely yellow flowers that accentuated her dark hair. The skirt flared full when she moved.

Philip halted halfway down the stairs. "What the hell?" he croaked, his voice thick with sleep.

The men stopped and straightened. Donna turned. The Aleut raised his eyebrows when he saw Philip. The large man coughed to cover a laugh. A bemused smile passed over Donna's mouth. The bathrobe Philip wore was Donna's, pink silk, and it came only to the middle of his skinny thighs.

"What's that, honey?" asked Donna.

"Exactly," said Philip, pointing. "What's that?'

"It's a piano," said Donna calmly. "Used. Tony's was selling it, and I've always wanted a piano. I thought you were at work."

Philip recognized the instrument from the bar downtown by the boat harbor. It was a player piano, with the same sort of metal coin tray used on Laundromat washing machines. Two quarters laid flat to make it play.

"Damn thing weighs a ton," said the large man on the porch. "Could use a hand getting it through the door."

Philip stared at them blankly. "I have to go to work," he said, and turned back up the stairs.

By the time he was dressed in brown corduroy pants and a black turtleneck, the piano had been installed in the living room, flush against the back wall, behind the ratty sofa. The men were in the truck, gunning the engine, rocking it back and forth to free the tires from the sucking mud. Nicholas cried. Philip leaned over the bassinet and regarded the child. Nicholas was smaller than he should have been, Philip thought.

"He's hungry," announced Philip. He could hear Donna moving in the kitchen, out of sight behind the half wall that separated the first floor of the A-frame. He eyeballed the diaper. "He's wet, too."

"I know," she called back. "I'm going to try again."

"I thought . . . I thought you were . . . I thought we were going to stick with bottles for now. I bought Enfamil."

"If I don't try, Carol will kill me. It's important, Phil."

Philip exhaled loudly. "I have to go to work."

Donna stepped back into view and lifted Nicholas without looking at Philip.

"A piano?" said Philip, his face sour and drawn.

"Do you want to talk about it?" Donna responded flatly.

"No," he said. "I'm late already."

Three Saints Hospital was a grim concrete building on the north edge of town. The military had built it to serve troops stationed on Kodiak during the Second World War, when Alaska was under attack. The hospital had been modernized in the thirty years since, but it remained squat and functional and unappealing.

Philip parked their rusting Pinto in the staff area behind the hospital and sat in the car for a moment, listening to the engine tick, pausing before the exertion of going inside. Within minutes the windows of the Pinto steamed opaque. Dampness was a feature of southwest Alaska. The constant drizzle seeped into everything. Philip felt as though he had never been fully warm or dry since moving to the island from New York six months before. The damp had seeped into his bones like vinegar, turning them to rubber, eroding him.

He stepped from the car and walked across the gravel parking lot, avoiding the brown puddles scummed with dull oil rainbows. The hospital was quiet when he entered. Only a few of the twenty-eight beds were occupied, unless anything had changed overnight. A collapsed lung, an elderly minor stroke, a post-op gallbladder. During summer the hospital bustled with the mangled hands and broken limbs of commercial fishermen. But now, in November, as the light dimmed toward winter, the only sound in the corridor was the echo of Philip's shuffling gait.

He passed the hushed nurses' station where two Filipino nurses sat watching a morning show on a small black-and-white television. Their chairs creaked as they both shifted in their starched white uniforms to watch him approach.

"Dr. Merlino's looking for you," said the one of the nurses. Violetta. She was the older of the two, perhaps in her late fifties. Thin and cranky. The tone of her voice was, as usual, clipped and minatory.

"I'm late, I know," said Philip. "I feel awful."

"You look bad," said the other nurse, Maria. "Baby keeping you up?"

"No," said Philip. "No. I'm just . . . just tired, I guess."

Violetta turned back to the television. "You better change and find Dr. Merlino," she said.

Philip skulked down the lime-green corridor to the staff room to put on his physician assistant scrubs. The staff room was cramped: half locker room and half crummy efficiency apartment, with a sink and a hotplate. An ugly pastel couch, a gift of the Ladies' Hospital Auxiliary, dominated the room. Philip changed slowly, fatigued by the effort. When he finally managed to put on his blue cotton uniform, he stumbled to the bathroom, leaning his forehead on the cool tile above the urinal.

The door opened behind him and Dr. Merlino unzipped, standing at the urinal next to Philip's.

"Hell have you been?" Dr. Merlino was a brusque man in his mid-forties, barrel-chested and short, with a well-groomed black beard turning gray around his chin. From Philip's first week on the island, Dr. Merlino had made it clear that he thought little of physician-extenders in general, and even less of Philip in particular.

"Sorry," mumbled Philip, not moving his head.

"You were on at six. I had to get Violetta to cover for you."

"I know. I'm just . . . I'm sorry."

Dr. Merlino's tone changed abruptly. "Well," he said, "that can't be good."

Philip opened his eyes. Dr. Merlino was staring into the bowl of Philip's urinal. Philip looked down. The liquid was dark brown and pungent, the color of well-steeped tea. "Oh," Philip said. "Oh dear."

Dr. Merlino reached over and flushed the urinal. He patted Philip on the back. "You look like shit," he said. "Let's get you worked up."

Hours later Philip was asleep on the Ladies' Auxiliary couch, knees pulled to his chest. He had picked up the phone to call Donna but fell asleep before she answered. Dr. Merlino had told him that he was likely infected with serum hepatitis B. The labs back from Anchorage would confirm it. He said that there would be no lasting damage, that he should rest, and his body would shake it off in a few weeks. A shot of gamma globulin. He ordered him to go home. The news did not startle Philip. Instead he felt a sudden sense of recognition, as though a mirror had been held up before him and he could see himself clearly and sink with relief into the fatigue he had been struggling to ignore. Through the slow progression of his illness he hadn't noticed anything amiss with his urine. The cabin had a chemical toilet, where all excretions disappeared into the fetid darkness of the waste chamber. After Dr. Merlino delivered the news, Philip remembered the drunken fisherman, red-faced and roaring, beard wet with spit, who tackled him in the exam room during a blood draw, leaving the needle stuck firmly in Philip's palm. He wasn't sure, but suspected that the fisherman had been the cause.

"Phil? Hey Phil, wake up." Maria shook him. The phone receiver blurted harshly and she replaced it to its cradle, silencing its noise with the depression of the switch hook.

"Phil?" She touched his shoulder gently and he waved her off with a grunt.

"What?"

"Merlino says go home."

Philip groaned and let his feet swing off the couch, giving him the momentum to sit upright. Maria stood over him, arms akimbo and mouth scrunched, eyeing him.

"You look bad. You go home and have soup. Tell your wife to make you a good soup. Something good for you. Mrs. Phil is a nurse, right?"

Philip stood shakily. "She was a candy striper."

"Why doesn't she work here if she's a nurse? Violetta doesn't want to work so much. She's old. Why doesn't Mrs. Phil work here?"

"Because she's at home with Nicholas."

"With the baby? I have two babies. You tell me."

Philip shrugged and Maria left. He still wore his scrubs but decided not to change. He put his street clothes into a brown paper bag and tucked it under his arm.

As he walked down the corridor to exit the hospital, a figure stumbled through the main doors. A short young woman with a pale face and hair that was clumped and matted in strange braids. She appeared dirty and panicked. She staggered into the reception area, slipping on the floor, almost falling and then catching her balance. Her clothes, wet with rain, clung to her body. Her belly was large and pregnant and the back of her rough patchwork skirt was dark with blood. Again she started to fall. "I am not okay," she said. Her voice was high and shaking. "I am not okay."

When Philip finally left the hospital, his scrubs were bloody from catching the woman. She collapsed unconscious just as he passed her, and he managed to hook his arms beneath her shoulders so that she fell back into him and her weight carried them both to the floor, as if they tried to sit in the same chair and found it pulled from beneath them. For a moment they lay on the black-and-white linoleum tile, Philip with his arms wrapped around her, cushioning her from the hard surface. Her solid and compact body was heavy against him. Her head, with its tangled mass of brown hair, rested on Philip's chest. He had focused on the twisted braids splayed across his shoulders, bristling against his neck. Some were decorated with shells and pumice stone and bits of driftwood, carefully tied and woven into her hair. Others matted to dreadlocks. They sat together on the floor until Maria and Violetta and the others came with a gurney and lifted her away. He could still smell the scent of her hair against his face as he walked out into the parking lot. It was an earthy scent, not clean, mixed with some perfume or oil. Lavender or sandalwood. It stirred something awake in him for a moment, pushed through his fatigue. It may have just been the adrenaline from the incident itself. He didn't notice the smear of blood on his pants until he sat down in the car.

It was a three-mile drive from the hospital to the A-frame in the woods. Most of the town of Kodiak clustered around the waterfront, dominated by the boat harbor and the canneries. On foot, one could discover most of what the town had to offer in about twenty minutes: a pizza parlor, ten bars, a single grocery store, a sporting goods outfitter, a ship chandlery. In the summer, the canneries packed salmon, crab, and shrimp day and night without cease. The docks were in constant motion with boats and cranes and forklifts and people in orange raingear working beneath haranguing clouds of gulls. The population of the town swelled by a third between May and September, adding another thousand or so people to the island. Most of the cannery workers were young, college kids or hippies, who lived in the cannery bunkhouses or camped in the tent city that blossomed every summer in the shadow of the BioDry—a fish waste rendering plant whose stench took getting used to.

Behind the waterfront, the town stretched out on irregular unpaved streets, leading to houses, the post office, the Fish and Game building, and nine churches. Mill Bay Road, the main road out of town, cut west across the northern tip of the island from the harbor past the hospital and then merged with Rezanof, which followed the jagged coast south for some ten miles before giving out just beyond the town dump. A bullet-pocked yellow sign marked the end of the road. Philip turned left out of the parking lot and headed home on the uneven dirt surface, weaving like a drunk around the infinite potholes.

He followed the road past the turn-offs to the elementary school and the adult-education center, both hidden behind the darkly knitted spruce forest. He passed the lumberyard and the grim trailer park where he and Donna almost lived before meeting Carol and finding the A-frame. Seeing the trailers through the trees, dented and rusting single wides, pained him. Alaska was not what he anticipated. It was not the simple frontier he imagined from the Saturday westerns. Instead of wilderness and moral clarity, he found himself in a shabby plywood-built fishing town as complicated in its workings as anywhere else. He recognized now that his impulse to flee to an isolated cabin in the woods had been absurd. Though he had brought himself and Donna here, insisted on it even, he felt that he had somehow been left behind.

The Pinto's tires rattled beneath him as he made the left onto Rezanof. Here the landscape opened up along the coast. The road skirted high black-rock cliffs and dipped almost to sea level over creeks running through corrugated steel culverts. To his right Philip could see the white-capped immensity of the Pacific crashing against the cliffs and rock beaches. The bleak winter sea. He passed a few trucks heading into town, some laden with piles of seine web, others empty after a trip to the dump. Most drivers lifted four fingers briefly from their steering wheels as they passed. The taciturn local greeting. After a mile of coast the road cut back into the forest, skirting around Fort Abercrombie State Park, a crumbling series of concrete bunkers and pillbox leftover from the coastal defenses of World War II. Half a mile beyond that, Philip eased off Rezanof onto the short dead end that led to the cabin.

148

He parked the Pinto at the foot of the driveway, not trusting it to reach the house without foundering in the mud. Carol's off-duty cab was parked at the bottom of the hill, as it often had been since the afternoon Carol first showed them the cabin. The cabin belonged to her brother, Edgar Carruth, a fisherman and then soldier who had stayed in Thailand after Vietnam, leaving Carol to rent the place out. Like many people in Kodiak, Carol seemed to have gigs everywhere: she drove a cab, bartended at Tony's, managed a few rentals, and, in her spare time, organized La Leche League meetings for new mothers. She and Donna took to each other right away.

Donna was more successful at making friends in Kodiak than she had been in New York. There, she had been one of millions, an unhappy Catholic girl from New Jersey. In Kodiak she was something of an exotic, a *New Yorker*, who wore heels instead of rubber boots, pantyhose instead of sweatpants, perfume instead of DEET. The role energized her and she adopted it with relish. She would speak of food and culture and fashion and nightlife as though she had been an Upper East Side debutante who decided to move to Alaska as a clever lark. She often began sentences with the phrase, "Well, in New York . . ." Philip said nothing to challenge Donna's elaborating mythology, or to hinder the arrogance growing along with it, though once during a dinner at the house of a new acquaintance, while she held forth on the Village art scene, Philip felt so suddenly infuriated that he abruptly pushed away from the table, causing his chair to topple back onto their hosts' elderly dachshund, breaking the dog's hind leg, and ending the evening in disaster. On the sullen drive home, Donna observed that the couple had a piano and that they seemed very cultured and that she had always wanted to learn to play.

Philip's success at making friends in Kodiak was limited. While Donna blossomed into her remade self, he collapsed into his own shadow. He did not expect to find the heady atmosphere he had tasted briefly in the Village, but early on he hoped that there would be a few like-minded men who shared his passions. Once in a bar he met a fat poet who railed against Robert Service and spoke of the need for "a new Alaskan poetics." Philip was delighted until the man became fully crocked and began to recite his own poems, which were awful. The man suggested that since Philip claimed to be a sculptor he should check out some of the Aleut carvings at the small historical museum down by the ferry dock. "Picasso ripped off the Natives," the man mumbled darkly after Philip's lukewarm response to the poems, "why not give it a try?"

The historical museum was housed in the former residence of an official of the Russian-American Company, a building from the late 1700s. It was a clapboard structure with a covered front porch where a man sat on a low bench most days, carving chunks of beach cedar. Philip approached him one afternoon and stood near the man to view his work. He was carving a mask, a teardrop-shaped mask with a human face but with an owly, beak-like mouth. The man's own face was wide and dark, with high, round cheekbones beneath eyes almost black. The man nodded at Philip when he approached but didn't speak.

"Is that an Aleut mask?" asked Philip, finally.

The man nodded and exhaled heavily through his nose.

"I'm a sculptor myself," said Philip. "Are you an Aleut?"

The man looked up at Philip, his eyes narrowed slightly. "I'm Russian," he answered in a low and even voice.

"Oh," said Philip, suddenly uncomfortable. "That's interesting."

The man turned his attention back to his work and Philip stood awkwardly for a moment before moving a few steps away, as if to take in the scenery. He unconsciously began to whistle an aimless tune. When he looked back the man had left.

Climbing the steep and muddy cabin driveway further exhausted him. In the long days of summer, the dense spruce forest around the cabin echoed with the songs of hermit thrushes and golden-crowned sparrows. Now the dark woods were silent but for the occasional croak of a raven and ceaseless dripping. The mud of the driveway froze in heaves at night and thawed in the rain of the day. The ruts left by the moving truck made negotiating a path even more difficult. Philip forgot to bring a jacket in the morning and by the time he stood on the porch his scrubs were soaked through. But the air smelled of wood smoke, and from the metal chimney he could see that Donna had a fire going.

When Philip opened the door he found Donna and Carol sitting on opposite sides of the squat black woodstove. The stove doors were open and its heat radiated out into the living room. Carol was on the couch, knitting something orange and purple that spilled across her lap from a canvas bag next to her. Donna sat in one of two upholstered chairs on the other side of the stove from the couch. Carol's two children, a boy of three and a girl of four, played with Lincoln Logs on the rag-weave rug between the two women.

The couch faced the front door and Carol saw Philip first, her eyes widening when she noticed the smeared blood on his clothing.

"Goodness, Phil," she said. "What happened to you? Donna, look at him."

Donna leaned forward in her chair and looked left over her shoulder. "Is that blood?"

Philip closed the door behind him and dropped into the other easy chair facing the couch. "Where's Nicholas?" he asked.

"He just went down," said Donna. "What happened? You look awful."

"It's not mine," he said, brushing his hands over his lap as though to clear the stains away. "It was some girl. She was coming in as I was leaving. A miscarriage."

"How terrible," said Carol, shaking her head. "How terrible. Who was she?" Carol, in small-town fashion, combined kind concern with a mercenary taste for gossip. Philip paused before answering.

"I didn't recognize her," he said. "Probably around twenty. A hippie, a bit unkempt. I'm not sure if it was a miscarriage. It just seemed that way. Maybe a stillbirth. She was pregnant, anyway. I didn't stay after she came in. Merlino told me to go home." Philip sighed deeply and looked at his hands. "Ordered me to, actually."

Donna's face clouded and she looked briefly at Carol, whose mouth tightened as an understanding passed between them. He realized that he had been the subject of conversation. "Because you were late again? You didn't get fired did you? I told you, didn't I? You can't just waltz into a job when the mood strikes you, Phil. I mean really, what—."

Philip waved his hand with an energy that surprised him and silenced her. "I didn't get fired. I'm not getting fired. Merlino told me to go home because I'm sick, which you haven't noticed, apparently." He stared at Carol who turned back to her knitting, suddenly engrossed in counting stitches. The edge in his voice alerted the children, who paused to assess the grownups. "It's medical leave. Paid, you'll be happy to hear. Seeing as how we have a new piano. Christ."

In the following silence, Carol's son moved to the couch and crawled up on her lap, displacing the knitting. The boy shoved her shirt up and began to nurse, while Carol recovered the knitting and began again. Philip had listened to Carol's La Leche lectures on the importance of breastfeeding, and the right of the child to direct the process, but the sight of a three-year-old doing so made him wince. He focused his gaze on the rug, where the girl was exploiting her brother's absence to gather all the Lincoln Logs into a pile before her.

"Medical leave?" asked Donna finally. "For what?"

Philip explained about the hepatitis, about the drunken fisherman, about how tired he felt. Donna listened to Philip speak with her head cocked to one side. Carol knitted head down. The boy finished nursing and returned to the rug to find his logs gone. He and the girl squabbled until Carol leaned forward and divided the piles evenly, making them both start over.

"Merlino wants you and Nicholas to go in tomorrow and get tested," Philip continued. "It's a quick test, just to see if you've been exposed. Then, you know, a shot of gamma globulin. It's nothing."

Donna maintained her head-cocked posture, pursing her lips as though she was turning the news over. "Well that's just super," she said. "You know how I get along with doctors." She shook her head meaningfully at Carol. A locum ob-gyn had prescribed Donna bromocriptine, and she held a grudge. Donna stood and walked to the piano, running her fingers along the keys.

"I can go with you," said Carol, helpfully. "I'm off tomorrow, and Dave will be home to watch the kids."

"Do you have a quarter?" Donna asked Philip without turning. "I thought I had some but I don't. Carol only had one. We need another for it to work."

Philip opened the shopping bag containing his street clothes and fished a quarter from his pants pocket, raising it up in the air for her to take. When she didn't turn, he said, "Here."

Donna took the quarter and sat on a kitchen chair before the piano. She slotted the coins into the tray and pushed them home with a metallic *kerchunk*. The change box had been removed so the coins simply clattered into an open cavity. Donna retrieved them and put them in her pocket. The piano gave a click and a whir, and then began to play. The song was the two-step Joplin rag "The Entertainer." The syncopated notes spilled out into the room and the keys moved, as though depressed by ghostly fingers.

Carol looked up from her knitting and spoke to the air. "It only has that one punch roll. You can't get other rolls for that model anymore, I guess. That's why the bar sold it. Everyone was sick of that song. It's like listening to an ice-cream truck."

"I like it," said Donna. "I won't even have to take lessons to play."

"I'm tired," said Philip. "I'm going to bed." He stood and climbed slowly up the stairs to the sleeping loft, back to the gritty mattress. Donna stayed at the piano, swaying slightly with her fingers poised above the moving keys as the music played.

After the song stopped, when Philip's head was pushed deeply in his pillow, he heard the hushed voices of the women talking in the room below, knowing that they were talking about him.

Philip awoke at noon. He had jumbled memories of Donna coming to bed, but he hadn't noticed when she left. It was quiet—the hollow silence of a house empty of people. The skylight blurred with vein-like rivulets, but it wasn't raining hard enough to sound on the roof. Philip felt a wave of nausea pass over him and his mouth filled with the nickel taste of spit. He curled onto his side and slept again.

Hours later he heard the front door open and then the sound of Donna downstairs. Philip roused himself and dressed slowly, his body stiff with sleep and sickness. He imagined his blood to be thick and unmoving, a muddy trickle insufficient to animate him. After dressing he had to sit back down on the bed to catch his breath. When he descended from the loft he found Nicholas wide-eyed and quiet on the couch and Donna setting up an air mattress that covered the entire floor of the small back room. "Everything go okay?" he asked.

Donna nodded and selected some bedding from a shelf. "I suppose. We both got shots. Nicholas fussed, but Merlino says that we'll be fine."

"Good. Sorry about all the hassle."

"It's not really your fault, is it?" She gave him a quick smile as she unfolded the sheets. "Though Merlino did say that you should have been more careful."

Philip shrugged. "So what's all this?"

"It's for Adele."

"Who's Adele?"

"She's the girl who miscarried. Me and Carol met her. It was an abruption. Thirty-two weeks, poor thing. Merlino kept her overnight, but she doesn't have any place to go. Carol was going to take her, but she doesn't have the room."

"But we don't even know her. That's crazy. What about the father?"

Donna stopped her preparations and squared her shoulders to Philip. "The father is gone. He apparently went back Down South months ago. She's on her own. And she's been living by herself in some old bunker in Abercrombie." Donna snapped a sheet in the air, letting it fall flat on the mattress. "I think I've even seen her hitchhiking before."

"But we don't even know her," Philip repeated, his voice rising.

"She's a very nice person. Both Carol and I thought so. She's homely, poor thing, but that doesn't mean no one should be kind to her. When we talked with her she was worn out. Almost like a robot, the way she talked. Like *Lost in Space*. Besides, with you being sick . . . I'll be taking care of you and Nicholas, and I could use the help."

"What do you mean, help? You can't just take someone in so that they'll be some kind of servant. We're both home."

"Philip," she interrupted him, her words coming quickly, "I may not always be home. I've signed up for Italian lessons at the Ed Center, twice a week. I may want to do other things, too. I have to stay busy or this place will drive me insane. Do you want to hire babysitters all the time? I can't keep asking Carol. You're apparently sleeping all day. You're the one who wanted to move here, remember. If we were back East, my mother would help, but we're not, so what do you want to do?"

"I've got to go to the bathroom," he said.

He shuffled past the couch and around the half wall, through the narrow kitchen and into the cold bathroom, which smelled sharply of white bar soap and damp. He brushed his teeth, scowling with his jaw clamped. Donna got under his skin and it made him feel stuck and enraged. To admit she was right had become impossible. The crushed bristles of the brush scraped on his gums and it hurt. He hunched his shoulders over the sink and spit. He washed his face. The well water coming through the faucet was orange with iron and it smelled like swamp gas, but it was cold and it felt good. He let it run and continued to splash it against his face until his cheeks went numb.

Donna stood in the kitchen, and he shuffled past her as he left the bathroom. She smiled at him and brushed her hand on his arm as he passed.

"Do you want some tea?" she asked. "You should be drinking a lot of fluids. Or I can heat up some soup if you're hungry. Have you eaten anything today?"

Philip stopped and nodded. "Tea would be good. I'm not really hungry." He pulled out a chair and sat at the small kitchen table. It was midafternoon and the daylight was already fading. The watery gray sky freezing into solid black.

"So when is she coming?" asked Philip. "This Adele."

"Oh, anytime now. Carol was going to help her check out and then get her stuff from the bunker. So anytime."

The water boiled and the kettle sounded. Donna poured the tea and set a mug in front of Philip and then sat down with her own across from him at the table. They drank in silence for a moment and then Nicholas began to cry.

"Well, if it doesn't work out," said Philip, as Donna stood to tend to the infant, "I'm reserving my objection. If it doesn't work out, she'll have to find someplace else, okay?"

"Of course," said Donna. "I feel the same way." She pushed back her chair and as she passed the front door she switched on the porch light.

In time they heard voices through the trees and then the stomping of shoes on the porch. Donna opened the front door and Carol entered, carrying a duffle bag and a backpack, followed by the girl from the hospital, Adele. Her hair was still heavy and braided, but her broad face had color and she smiled shyly. The scent of her, the outdoors, the cold, pushed in behind them.

Carol dropped the bags on the floor. "We got everything out of the bunker. I can't believe anyone would live there. Really, Adele." Carol reached and rubbed Adele's back reassuringly.

Adele gave a little shrug, a small gesture. "In summer there are many people who live there," she said. Her voice was airy, almost a whisper, but she sounded each word precisely. Carol lingered briefly before saying her good-byes and heading off into the darkness with a borrowed flashlight to navigate down the driveway.

"Well, welcome," said Donna, hugging Adele awkwardly. "I'm glad you're staying with us. This is my husband, Phil."

Philip stood from the table and reached out his hand. She took it gently.

"Yes. You are the man who caught me," she said. "I remember."

"How're you feeling?" Philip asked.

"I am still very tired," she answered.

"You can rest here," said Donna. "Why don't you get settled in?"

Donna tended to Nicholas and heated some soup while Philip made the fire. Adele unpacked in the back room and then came and sat on the couch, her legs tucked up beneath her. When the fire had caught, Philip sat back on the rug and stared at the flames, blinking slowly.

"You are very weary, too," said Adele.

"Yes. I am," he answered. "I've got . . . I caught some bug and I'm trying to shake it. It makes me exhausted." He paused and felt himself flush slightly. "But it's nothing compared to what you went through. I'm sorry."

"No," she said placidly. "It is different. I did not have a bug."

Philip looked up at her. She was staring into the fire as well. "I'm sorry that you went through that," he said. "It must have been awful." She gave a slight nod. "After dinner," he continued, "you should get some rest. I'm going to, so don't feel shy about it. You need to sleep."

"Yes," she said. "I think I will sleep."

From the kitchen, Donna announced dinner. As they sat she apologized to Adele. "It's just tomato soup and cheese sandwiches.

I'm not much of a cook, but I'm learning to do more." Adele smiled at her softly and gave her small shrug. "Anyway," said Donna, "you can't really buy anything good at the grocery store. Everything always seems to be moldy or wilted or in cans. I guess it has to travel so far to get here. On barges and whatnot." She paused, watching for Adele's reaction, "Not like New York."

Adele smiled again. "It is very nice of you and Philip to have me here for now," she said simply.

Philip nodded dismissively. "Happy to," he said.

"Where are you from, Adele?" asked Donna. Her voice shifted, becoming businesslike and prim, like an interviewer. "Where did you grow up?"

Adele chewed a bite of sandwich slowly and did not answer until she had swallowed and taken a sip of water. "I am from Fresno, California," she said. She enunciated every syllable in turn, as though it was a song.

"What brought you here?"

Adele swallowed a mouthful of soup and set the spoon back with a precise intention. "I came here with the church," Adele said finally. "To come with the church to work in the cannery."

"Oh really?" asked Donna. "What church was that?"

Adele gave her shrug again and smiled. "I do not really belong to it anymore."

"We shouldn't pester her with questions," said Philip. "She's been through a lot."

"I didn't mean to pester," replied Donna quickly, eyes narrowed on Philip. "Just making conversation."

Adele looked at them both, her face placid and unchanged. From the cradle, Nicholas began to fuss uncomfortably. Donna let her spoon clatter in her empty bowl and went to tend to him. Adele's face blanched as she listened to the infant's noises, and then Donna's voice soothing him back into silence.

"I'm sorry," said Philip. "It must be hard to be here, with a . . . Well, you know. It must be hard."

Adele tilted her head slightly and her placid expression returned. "No. It must not be hard. It was not right for me to have a baby. I was in the wrong position."

"Well," said Philip. They finished their meal in silence, and Philip cleared the plates when they were done. With Nicholas quiet again, Donna ran the quarters through the piano twice. She held her fingers as before, just above the jumping keys. Adele sat on the couch and listened to "The Entertainer," while Philip crawled up to bed where he fell asleep without undressing.

Philip awoke to the scent of pancakes and the murmurs of the women talking in the kitchen below. Donna's voice was quick and cheerful, punctuated with explosive little laughs. Adele's voice was the same: soft and precise and strange, with some words drawn out, their syllables nearly extended into song. Philip felt hungry for the first time in days.

Adele stood over the range watching the pancakes as Philip came down from the loft. Donna held Nicholas in one arm and cleared a few dirty plates from the table with the other.

"I'm going to cut Adele's hair today," said Donna, grinning. "A bob, maybe. Or a pageboy like mine. Or maybe no bangs." She stepped next to Adele and held out one of the twisted braids in her hand. "Don't you think? Something shorter?"

Philip pursed his lips and raised his eyebrows noncommittally. "Not really my area," he said.

"Oh but we have to," said Donna with an explosive laugh. "Feel this braid, Phil. Feel how heavy it is."

Philip hesitated and then reached, holding the extended hair briefly between his fingers and thumb. He felt suddenly awkward and let the braid fall back onto Adele's shoulder. "Not really my area," he repeated.

Adele turned, sliding a stack of pancakes onto a plate. "Are you hungry, Philip?" she asked. "We have already eaten."

Philip nodded and the awkward sensation returned. "These look delicious," he said. When he absentmindedly brushed his hand over his face before eating, he caught the faint scent of Adele lingering from her hair, the same scent he had noticed in the hospital. He chewed his food slowly.

Donna and Adele left him alone at the table and sat down near the woodstove, some ten feet away. Donna sat in the easy chair, with Nicholas on her lap, and Adele sat on the couch, with her legs tucked beneath her. They sat in silence for a moment, with no sound in the cabin but for the scrapes Philip made on his plate.

"Sorry we don't have a television or anything," said Donna. "The days can get long here. Do you like to read? We have books."

Adele nodded slowly. "Yes. Sometimes I like to read."

"Well here then," said Donna, standing. "Take Nicholas for a second. I'll find you a book." She set Nicholas down on Adele's lap and stood back a step as Adele adjusted him. Nicholas laid still and quiet, bound up in a blanket. "There you are," said Donna, nodding. "Just like that." She went over to the low bookcase beneath the stairs.

Philip sat at the table, his plate smeared brown with syrup, and watched Adele hold Nicholas. Her face was intent, focused on the infant. He noticed uncomfortably that there were two wet stains on her loose cotton shirt. Donna returned with two books in her hand and set them beside Adele. She observed her for a moment and then sat back into her chair.

"Your milk came in," said Donna quietly.

"Yes, it has. It feels very strange."

"Mine came in but there was never very much. And then it just seemed to dwindle away, even after I stopped taking that stupid pill. Carol kept after me to keep trying to nurse, but then it just got painful so I stopped."

"Yes. I can see how it would be painful. It is almost painful for me now. It aches. I feel it."

"You can try, if you want. With Nicholas. It might help. It might be good for the both of you."

"I'm not so sure about that," said Philip, alarmed, looking over his plate, holding a fork in his hand.

"Oh Phil, calm down," said Donna, a light smile in her voice. "This is between us women. Finish your pancakes."

Adele hesitated a moment and then lifted her shirt, pulling Nicholas to her. He seemed to struggle briefly before latching on. Adele's eyes widened and then closed and a strange expression passed over her face, a keenness that melted slowly as the minutes passed in silence. She sat unmoving while Nicholas nursed.

"I'll make some tea," said Donna. "And when we're done, I'll cut your hair."

The women went outside to the porch for the haircutting. Philip rinsed his plate and left it in the sink. He checked on Nicholas, who was fast asleep in his crib. The sight of Adele nursing unnerved him, but Nicholas seemed full and content. Philip's own stomach was warm with breakfast and he felt heavy and drowsy. He slouched onto the couch, moving aside the books Donna had selected. One was *Jonathan Livingston Seagull*, the other was *Surfacing*. He hadn't read either, though he had given Donna the Bach book as a gift during the two weeks they dated, back when they shared the night shift at St. Luke's Hospital. Before he called it off. Before she had tearfully announced her pregnancy, her face red with despair, saying she had been praying on her knees and could not have an abortion. Before he had married her and fled to Alaska to escape their families and attempt a fresh start somewhere unknown. A jagged island in the sea, set apart from the world. Where, he had imagined, they could regroup in the clarity of the wilderness.

Philip flipped through the book, looking at the pages but not reading. He considered making a fire to take the chill off the still air in the cabin, but he saw that the woodbox was empty and decided against it. He dozed.

Donna woke him some time later, pushing at his shoulder. "Nice nap?" she asked. "We're cold. Can you get a fire going?"

"What time is it?" He sat upright and rubbed his face.

"It's around one. Adele's taking a shower. Her hair was a mess and it took forever, but it's better now. We don't have any wood in here."

Philip stomped into his boots and headed outside. The air was cold and fresh after the stillness indoors. He leaned on the porch railing and breathed deeply, inhaling the damp earthy scent of spruce forest and moss, a scent spiced with growth and decay. The firewood was stacked in a long pile beneath the porch to keep it dry. He made several trips up and down the stairs, filling the woodbox and then stacking some larger wedges on the floor by the stove. He was feeling better than he had for a while. Perhaps it was the nap and then the exercise of hauling wood, or maybe it was the chill in the afternoon air. He set aside a few straight-grained chunks of wood and carried them to the stump he used as a chopping block. He split the chunks into thin sticks of kindling with precise swings of the ax. It was a task that he enjoyed. He liked to look at a chunk of wood and guess the hidden contours of the grain, the way the wood wanted to split. He liked the smooth passage of the ax that proved his sense of the wood was right. It was like looking at a chunk of marble and seeing the sculpture inside.

Philip collected the sticks of kindling that had fallen around the chopping block. Though winded, he felt good. The wood put him in mind of marble, and he decided to spend some time in his studio. He cradled the kindling in one arm while he dragged the ax back to the porch and set it on the woodpile, out of the rain. He brought the kindling in and got the fire going in the stove, easing a match around the edges of crushed newspaper until the wood caught. Donna sat on the rug with a tackle box full of cosmetics, picking out different bottles of nail polish and arranging them on the floor. Adele was still in the bathroom, though he could hear that the shower had stopped.

"We're gonna paint our nails," she said.

"Okay," Philip answered. "I'll be in the studio for a bit."

Donna nodded and continued to line up her bottles. Philip set a large log on the growing fire and closed the stove doors. He stood and set the damper.

"This should be good for a while," he said.

The studio, as Philip called it, was a shed behind the cabin. It was a small corrugated metal building backed into the trees. There wasn't much to it, just a workbench and an old vinyl-top card table. Edgar

Carruth had used it to store his nets and other commercial fishing gear. Carol had sold what she could and the remainder was mostly junk: moldering coils of rope, engine parts coated with oil and dust, a large screwdriver with a bent shaft. Philip shoved it to a back corner to clear a space for himself.

At Duke, Philip had quit pre-med and taken a degree in sculpture instead, hoping to find success in New York but willing to fall back on his physician's assistant certificate if he didn't. Once in New York, Philip was taken by the minimalists and their shiny symmetries. He loved the boozy Village conversations about ambient space and implicating the viewer. He met sculptors and photographers and painters. He stood next to them and their intimates at gallery openings and raucous after-parties in smoky downtown apartments. He still repeated their names to himself often—*Sol LeWitt, Robert Smithson, Eva Hesse*—reminding himself how close he had been to them, their names as smooth as sea-glass in his mouth.

But in Kodiak his thoughts drifted back to the figurative work that captured him in the first place: the ancient Greeks, Michelangelo, Rodin, even the monuments of Marshall Fredericks he saw growing up near Detroit. He duct-taped a water-stained print of the *Dying Slave*, cut from a garage-sale book on the High Renaissance, above the workbench. Philip couldn't get marble, or much else, to work with. But he made sketches and sometimes bought clay or soapstone from the pottery teacher at the Ed Center. It was important to him to continue, even though he had fallen back on his certificate, even though he felt that he was still falling.

He left the door of the shed open to allow for light and stood before the workbench, looking over his last efforts. For the past months he had been working on a collection of clay figures, two adults and two children, who were to stand together naked, holding hands. In his mind he called it the *Burghers of Kodiak*, but he couldn't get any of the figures right and the composition felt forced and insincere. He moved the figures aside, setting them on the card table, and he took his sketch pad out of the plastic bag he kept it in to protect it from damp. He sat on a stool, hunched over the paper, and sketched.

Time passed and the steady beat of rain on the shed roof slackened. The surge of energy Philip felt earlier faded, and he sat motionless, staring at a new sheet of blank paper, rubbing the charcoal dust from his fingers. The weak afternoon sun dimmed and he reached to light the Coleman lantern he kept on the workbench. The white-thread mantle flared and he turned it down to a soothing hiss. He listened to it with attention and then turned back to the paper. He was sitting this way, hunched and staring blankly, when a soft rap sounded on the open door of the shed.

"Hello, Philip," said Adele. "Am I bothering you?"

Philip straightened his back and rubbed his face, leaving a thin smear of charcoal on his forehead. "No," he answered. "I'm stopping for now, I think. Getting tired. Aren't you painting nails or something?" Adele's twisted braids, the bits of wood and pumice stone, were gone. Her hair was short and straight, framing her face. Her features seemed larger, her nose more prominent, her bumpy forehead and blemished skin more obvious. But her brown eyes seemed to have grown larger, too, and her jaw more distinct. Philip was surprised that Donna had made such a successful job of it.

Adele crinkled her nose. "The smell of the polish does not agree with me."

"I don't blame you. I don't like it either." Philip motioned to a white plastic deck chair by the table. "Come and sit down if you want."

Adele sat.

"Are you feeling better?" he asked.

"Yes thank you. I am very grateful to you and Donna for being so kind to me."

"It's nothing. Besides, she likes the company." From the house "The Entertainer" cranked up again, its bouncing notes distorted by distance.

Adele cocked her head and stared at him frankly. It made him feel uncomfortable. "Do you still have family in Fresno?" he blurted. Adele continued to look at him and then she shifted her gaze to the table.

"Who are these people you are making?" she asked.

"They were a family that used to live here. In a nice house, downtown, near the Russian church. One day this summer, before the Fisherman's Festival, they came out of their house and stood naked on their lawn, and I saw it from across the street. They went crazy, I guess. Or something. Small town and all. It stuck in my mind."

"They seem very sad." She reached and cupped her hand around the shoulders of one of the figures, tipping it back as though to lay it down on the table.

"Yeah," said Philip nodding. "I think they were. I can't get it right though. I'm glad you see it."

Adele paused before she spoke, as she always seemed to do. "Why do you want to remind people that they have been sad?"

"I don't know," Philip laughed uncomfortably. "It's art, I guess. Isn't it? I'm just making something. Trying to make something beautiful."

"But you have already," she said.

It was Philip's turn to pause, to furrow his brow. "What do you mean?" he asked.

"Nicholas," said Adele. "You've already made someone beautiful who came naked into the world. Isn't he enough?"

Philip nodded and coughed. "You didn't answer my question," he said. "About Fresno. Do you still have family there?" Adele paused, and for a moment, Philip was irritated with her for pausing.

"Yes. I think I do. My mother. But it was not pleasant. Growing up with her." Adele's voice seemed to stay the same, even and precise, like pebbles being dropped one by one into water.

"So why did you come to Alaska? What brought you here?" Philip spoke impatiently.

Again Adele paused. "I said so already," she said tightly. "I came to Kodiak with the church. To come with the church to work in the cannery."

Philip felt sorry for pushing and looked down at his knees. There was silence in the shed, just the hissing of the lantern and the intermittent rain on the roof. When he raised his head, Adele was looking back at him with her eyes wide open, staring at him like a strange bird, like an appraising parrot.

"I'm sorry," he said. "I'm just curious. I don't even really know why I'm here. Or why I thought I wanted to come here. So why should you." He shifted awkwardly on his stool and looked at his hands.

Adele pursed her lips in thought, as though she was about to whistle, and then let a side of her mouth curl into a smile. Her body relaxed and something like amusement passed over her face. "That's all right, Philip," she said easily. "I don't mind. You can ask me."

"So what church was it? That you came here with."

"The Unification Church," she said simply.

"You're a Moonie?"

"I was a Moonie." Her voice flattened and she gave her little shrug. "I don't . . . do not know if I am still."

"Did you get married in one of those big ceremonies?"

"No, I was just in the beginning. You do not get married at the beginning." She looked down into her lap and smoothed her skirt over her thighs with a slow gesture. Then she told about growing up in Fresno with her unstable mother, leaving home when she was sixteen, and making her way to San Francisco with a friend. After the friend went back home, Adele drifted around the Bay Area for a difficult time before she was approached by members of the church. "I went to the three-day class and it was very nice. And then I went to the one-week class and then the two-week class, and they were very nice, too. So I joined." The church sent thirty of them to work in its new cannery in Kodiak. No witnessing, just work and fellowship.

"We all lived together in the bunkhouse," she continued. "There were many hugs. Always many hugs and closeness. Jared was the house leader. He was from Connecticut. Once Jared and I hugged each other, and it became something else. When I knew I was pregnant he was very cold. They were all very cold. They said that I was a danger to the Family. I broke the pure love pledge and was to be expelled. I was in a very narrow position. I was meant to be in the church as tight as a screw so that I could not be loosened. But I was not so tight. So I went with the baby in my belly to the tent camp. It smells bad there, but I slept and slept. Some days I sold flowers like I did in San Francisco, but I kept the money which I should not have done. I lived in the tent and tried to stay dry. The many people who lived in the tents shared until the summer was over and they left. So I moved to the concrete box because it was dry and no one was near. Then I was bleeding and went to the hospital and after that you know."

"That must have been difficult," Philip said. "Living alone in the woods at the fort, with no one."

"It was lonely sometimes. But the True Father said that John the Baptist did the same. He lived in the wilderness eating nuts and honey. Just like a hippie, he said." She smiled at that.

"The True Father? Is that Moon?"

Adele nodded. "Yes, he is the True Father. He is the Lord of the Second Advent."

Philip coughed. "That's a bit much, don't you think. Calling yourself lord?"

Adele fixed him with the same appraising look that had made him uncomfortable before. It wasn't angry, or even really critical, but just an expression of frank scrutiny, as though he had puzzled and disappointed her. "Was there ever a time when your family took responsibility for the salvation of the world?" she asked. "Have you ever awakened during the night and thought of your brothers and sisters, missing them and feeling compassion for them?"

Philip wasn't sure if the questions were rhetorical, but when she seemed to be waiting for an answer he shook his head. He felt the urge to cross his arms but resisted it.

"The True Parents have done such things. Right now, 1973, is the most tense time in the history of restoration. The True Father is a dispensational figure. This period of time cannot exist again."

"How's that?"

"We are at the end of the world."

"Well," said Philip, snorting. He crossed his arms. "I'd agree with that."

Adele's face clouded. "You do not listen," she said. "You do not think to create an exemplary family to solve the problems of the world. How do you feel about these tragedies? You do not know."

Philip watched Adele speak and uncrossed his arms. Her face had an intense sheen upon it. Philip was drawn to her. His legs twitched; his whole body trembled. His skin felt hot, flushed. He stood, pushing the stool away with his legs, wanting to say something that he did not know and could not articulate. And Adele kept him in her gaze, opening her eyes to him.

There was a rap at the shed door. "Interrupting anything?" said Donna, pushing in.

Philip startled and fumbled behind for the stool, adjusting it and sitting again. "No," he said. "No, we were just talking." He coughed loudly. "What time is it?"

"Almost six." Donna hesitated, her eyes swept tensely from Adele to Philip and back again. "What do you want to do about dinner?"

"I haven't thought about it. Anything would be fine."

"I defrosted some hamburger. We can have meatloaf. Or burgers."

"Fine," said Philip. Then he turned his face to Adele but did not look at her. "Is that okay with you Adele? Do you like meatloaf?"

Adele nodded. "I will come help you."

"Good," said Donna crisply, turning back to the house. Adele followed.

Philip sealed his sketchbook back into its plastic bag and snuffed the lantern. He sat alone in the darkened shed for a time, listening to the rain on the roof and the rising wind moaning through the surrounding forest like an encompassing animal.

Donna kept silent while making dinner, moving briskly and clattering dishes. Philip stoked the fire and sat by the stove, warming his hands after the chill of the shed. Adele held Nicholas, walking him in small bouncing circles, crooning to him softly. Philip did not recognize the song.

"I think he is hungry," said Adele, moving next to Donna. "I can make him a bottle if you like."

Donna turned briefly to examine Nicholas and then went back to the bowl of hamburger meat and breadcrumbs. "Sure," she said. "Everything's on the counter. Or you can nurse him yourself if you want. I don't mind."

Adele hesitated, as though trying to read Donna's meaning by staring at the back of her head. "All right," she said softly. She took Nicholas to the couch, sitting across from Philip, and began to nurse. She held Nicholas to her closely, rocking gently, her eyes shut.

Philip's gaze darted to Adele several times. He tried to focus on the fire but then stood up. "I'm going to take a quick shower before dinner," he announced as he passed Donna on the way to the bathroom.

There was not much conversation at dinner. It was pitch black outside and the windows mirrored in. The atmosphere of the cabin seemed tense and muted. The meatloaf was dry and the potatoes were nearly raw, but Philip praised the meal enthusiastically in an effort to cut the gloom. Neither of the women responded, so he let the atmosphere have its way and finished his meal in silence.

Philip cleared the table and washed the dishes while Donna and Adele sat reading by the fire. Outside, the wind strengthened, with occasional gusts rattling the walls. The temperature dropped. Philip felt a wave of nausea and when it passed he felt his strength ebb too. He leaned against the counter as the fatigue returned, drying his hands slowly.

"I'm going to bed," he announced. "I don't feel well."

Donna looked up from her book. "I think I'll lie down and read. I'm feeling sort of tired too."

Philip climbed to the loft and collapsed into bed. His body ached and he wondered if he was developing a fever. When Donna come up the stairs and undressed he rolled to face the opposite wall. He felt the weight of her as she sat on the mattress. She switched on the reading lamp and adjusted herself under the covers. He pushed down into the pillow and raised his arm to cover his face.

"The light bother you?" she asked. Philip did not reply. "Are you asleep?"

"No," he said after a moment, his voice muffled by the pillow. "I just don't feel well."

"Do you have a fever?" She reached her arm over and held her wrist against his forehead. "You're warm."

"I just need to sleep," he said.

He felt the shift of her body as she put her book down and turned off the light. Then she lay back still, unmoving. Philip could feel her alertness, could almost picture her staring at the ceiling. He pushed deeper into his pillow and brought his knees up to his chest.

Finally she broke her silence and whispered, "What do you think of her?"

He did not respond, and she nudged him.

"Phil. What do you think of her?"

He sighed. "She's a very strange girl," he said.

"I saw your face, the way you were looking at her. Do you think she's attractive?"

Adele was moving below them, getting ready for bed. He thought of her in the shed. Her eyes open to him, the line of her jaw above her neck. "No," he answered.

"I don't believe you."

He cleared his throat.

"She was out at the shed for a long time. What were you talking about?"

Philip straightened and rolled onto his back impatiently. "Nothing. I was just asking her how she was feeling. She's been through a lot."

"You never invite me out to the studio, to see what you're working on." Her voice rose slightly above a whisper and then she modulated it down again.

"You're never interested. Besides, I didn't invite her. She just showed up. What could I do? Not talk to her? You're the one who brought her here."

"Do you want me to ask her to leave?"

"It's a little late for that."

Donna was silent for a time, breathing in the dark. Philip considered rolling back over, then she spoke again. "Why do you say she's strange?"

"I don't know. The way she talks." He paused. "She's a Moonie, you know."

"A what? I don't even know what that is."

"And what's with her nursing Nicholas?" continued Philip. "That's a little strange, you encouraging that."

"Carol said it would be good for Nicholas and her. For both of them. It's natural. Better than formula."

Philip swallowed his comments on Carol. "I'm tired," he said.

Donna turned to him in the darkness and placed her hand on his chest. "I love you, Phil," she said. "You know that, don't you? I love you and Nicholas more than anything."

Philip breathed deeply, feeling Donna's hand rise and fall on his chest. "I know," he said.

The next morning they mixed a pitcher of Milkmaid and had cereal for breakfast. The temperature dropped during the night and the

174

branching frost was thick on the windows. Adele slept until late and when she came out of her room, smoothing down her new haircut, Donna was already dressed. Philip was at the table, finishing his cereal.

"I'm going into town," said Donna, addressing them both. "Carol says that Kinney's got a new shipment of shoes. We're going to take a look and then have lunch. I'm taking the car, Phil. I'll be back later on."

Adele nodded and Philip, mouth full, raised his spoon in good-bye.

"And Adele," said Donna, putting on her coat by the door, "Nicholas is fussing. He's hungry, if you wouldn't mind."

Adele stood frozen for a moment, halfway to the kitchen, next to Nicholas's crib. "Of course," she answered. She lifted Nicholas out and went to the couch. Donna left, closing the door firmly behind her. Philip listened to her shoes echo on the porch and then let his spoon drop into his bowl.

"Adele," he said. "You don't have to . . . do that. We can get a bottle going. Come and have some breakfast."

"It is all right, Philip." She did not look up as she spoke. "I understand."

Philip stood, pushing back his chair. He walked into the living room and positioned himself across from Adele. His hair was still rumpled with sleep and he was barefoot, dressed in the jeans and T-shirt he found near the bed when he awoke. He had made a fire when he got up, and now he busied himself adding logs and poking at it.

"What do you mean, you understand?" he asked. "You're our guest. Not some kind of . . . wet nurse or something."

Adele kept her gaze down at Nicholas. "Then you do not understand," she said evenly. "I am in a very narrow position as I must be."

"Then no, I don't understand," said Philip.

"*Even though I am become Satan,*" she said, in a voice that signaled a quotation, "*you have to love me.* That is what the archangel accuses."

Philip turned away from the fire and faced her, but her gaze did not shift. A rising shriek of steam escaped from the damp firewood, ending in a pop.

"I am like your piano, am I not? I have been brought here to sing in this way. But there is still love there and there is no purpose disturbing it."

"I have no idea what you're talking about," said Philip. "What you say doesn't make any sense."

Adele looked at Philip directly. "You are not good," she said.

"What are you talking about?"

"I will become more serious and then you will have to cry."

"What?"

"I have seen you, Philip. Philip and Donna. You have learned about each other and not so much remains there now. You do not see or smell her. You only wave skinny gestures at each other." She shifted Nicholas to her other breast. "No. Not so much remains there now."

"I don't even . . ." His breath trailed off in exasperation. "What the hell does that even mean?"

"That is what the archangel accuses," she repeated, as though in explanation. She raised Nicholas up onto her shoulder and rubbed his back. "One exemplary family can solve the problems of the world. You are not serious about love."

Philip shook his head, raising his arms and then letting them fall in a gesture of bewilderment. "Fine," he said. "Fucking Christ. Have at it. There's cereal on the table. Make yourself at home. I'm going to the studio." He thrust his bare feet into a pair of stiff leather boots and pulled on a sweater and a jacket. Without turning to look at Adele, he closed the door behind himself and stomped off to the shed.

Philip stayed in the shed for several hours. It was cold and he could not work, but he refused to return to the house. Instead, he paced the narrow floor, listening to the hiss of the lantern and thinking of Adele. He could hear her voice, and see her face before him, and he could not shake it. He felt his body wanting to pull toward her and a dull note of caution sounded in his head. He still felt a bit feverish and woozy but considered calling Merlino to ask whether he could come back to work. It would be a way to step outside the thickening atmosphere he felt growing around him, bearing down. But there was something about her that stirred him, inexplicable as she was. He remembered holding her as she fell, the sense of something awakening in him for a moment, pushing through his fatigue. It felt urgent to him, and he did not want to leave it alone. Finally, he shuttered the lantern and went back to the cabin.

He found Adele on the couch by the fire when he returned. She had dressed and combed her hair and was reading a book with her legs tucked beneath her. Nicholas made small contented sounds in his bassinet next to her. Philip kicked off his boots and hunched next to the stove, warming himself.

"It's gotten cold out there. I'm glad you aren't in that bunker anymore."

Adele turned the book down on her lap, open over her thigh. She nodded.

"Look, Adele," he began, "I'm sorry I was so, well, whatever, earlier. It's just that me and Donna haven't . . . well, it's always been difficult. And this . . . being sick. Being so tired. I'm not myself."

Adele nodded again. "I spoke wrongly. It is my task now to be honest and precise. But sometimes I say too much. Let us not speak of it."

"Good," said Philip, nodding. "I'd rather not."

"It is very nice and quiet here by the fire. We do not have to speak of anything."

Philip found a book to read and sat. They whiled away the afternoon comfortably. They read and chatted and any evidence of the earlier friction between them dissipated. Philip napped and occasionally stoked the fire. Adele nursed Nicholas when he was hungry, rocking him in her arms. Hours passed. When the daylight dimmed, Philip remembered that there were some Christmas lights in a box in the back room. He proposed putting them up around the windows. "I've always thought they give a good, snug feeling when it's dark," he said in unneeded explanation. He found the box and they untangled the strings and checked the bulbs. He grinned at her several times while they worked at it and she answered him with a reserved smile of her own. Once around the windows, the glow of the lights added to the peace and contentment Philip felt. He sat back down and stared into the fire.

"It's very nice, isn't it?" he asked.

"Yes, Philip," Adele answered. "It is very nice."

It was after eight o'clock when the silence of the house was broken by Donna coming up the porch stairs. She opened the front door in a flurry of shopping bags and packages that she dropped in a heap as she took off her coat. A punching burst of cold air followed her.

"Hey, hey," she said. Her face was flushed and she was breathing heavy. "How's everyone?"

The abruptness of her entry took Philip and Adele by surprise. Philip put his book down. "Hi," he said softly. "How was your day?"

"Great," said Donna. "Got some new shoes that I needed." She extended one leg out so that Philip and Adele could see the shoes. They were sandal-like pumps with cork heels. "They were half off because they're for summer, but I don't care. I've been wearing them all day. Very New York." She was speaking loudly, as though she was slightly buzzed.

"Very nice," said Philip, noncommittally.

"You put up the lights," she said. "I wish you would have asked me. I wanted those to go outside."

Philip shrugged. "It was just something to do."

"Well never mind," said Donna. "Carol and Dave are on their way up. I invited them over for dinner."

"Oh," Philip's face clouded. "I didn't know. I guess. I'm a little tired."

"Well I've already talked to them. They're bringing salmon or halibut or something. Dave just caught some. They ran home to pick it up. They're bringing wine, too. And I got some more." She raised a skinny brown bag triumphantly. "We just have to make a side. I'll make some rice or something."

"Okay. I mean, why even ask," Philip stammered. "Just, okay. Fine."

"They're probably parking the car by now. You should go help them carry stuff. Make sure to bring a flashlight. I almost fell on the way up."

"Sure," said Philip, standing reluctantly, irritated, and putting on his boots. He glanced at Adele, but her attention was focused on the fire.

Walking down the driveway, Philip heard the slam of car doors and the voices of Dave and Carol coming through the darkness. Philip did not like Dave. He was the bluff sort of Alaskan man who intimidated Philip, made him feel even more out of place than he already was. Dave worked for Fish and Game. During the summer, he flew around the bush checking salmon escapements or making sure seiners were within boundaries and all manner of things that Dave expected Philip to understand but that he never really did. When he wasn't working he was fishing or hunting for his own freezer. Dave was tall and thick and bearded and had sandy blond hair just beginning to show gray. His voice boomed at Philip from a distance down the driveway.

"Hey, Phil, how the hell are ya?"

"Good, Dave. Nice to see you. Need a hand?"

"Nah. I got it. Carol might though. Need a hand, Carol?"

Carol giggled and let out a snort. "Sure, that would be great."

Philip took the tearing grocery sack of wine and bread from Carol and handed her the flashlight.

"So what do you think of these ladies going out and getting tanked in the afternoon, huh?" Dave's tone was light and playful.

"Oh hell," Carol said, "we didn't get tanked. I just had to stop in at work for an hour and we had a few shots is all."

Dave laughed. "We got to catch up." He slapped Philip on the shoulder and stayed with him, walking close. "Can you believe that Nixon horseshit? 'I'm not a crook'? Who the fuck does he think he's kidding? And I even voted for the sonofabitch. Before what I knew what that bastard did to Begich and Boggs."

Philip paused. "I don't know. Is that what he said?"

"They don't have television, Dave. Phil doesn't sit for hours doing nothing like you."

"I don't blame you. Probably smart. Country going to hell, who wants to hear about it?"

"Where are the kids?" Philip felt suddenly ashamed for asking, knowing it to be a transparent nudge for Carol and Dave to go home.

"Got a babysitter. Good to have a night off. When yours gets older you'll appreciate it. Carol says you've got one living with you now. Damn good idea." He gave a short, knowing laugh. "Wish I'd thought of it."

"She's not really a babysitter," said Philip. "She just needs a place to stay until she gets back on her feet."

"Whatever you say, buddy."

Once inside, the conversation continued, growing louder and progressively more wine soaked. Donna and Carol swapped town gossip and cackled. Carol said that the Bowers finally got their kids back from Family Services and wasn't it all too sad, and then they laughed over the naked spectacle on the lawn. Dave lectured Philip on the subject of reloading ammunition, describing his new centerfire metallic press in great detail for nearly half an hour before Philip had any idea of what he was talking about. Donna fed the quarters into the piano and "The Entertainer" spun out again and again. She and Carol tried on each other's new shoes and made little staggering steps like they were at a ragtime disco. Dave went to the bathroom and announced that he had discovered a leak under the sink and insisted on giving Philip a plumbing lesson, even lumbering back down to his car for tools, because it was something every man ought to know. "That's right," said Donna, laughing. "Teach him, Dave." Adele refused any wine and sat uncomfortably on the couch with a glass of Tang made with the swampy well water. No one seemed sure of how to include her in the evening and as she remained silent she became invisible to them. Philip wanted to sit next to her and put his arm around her and reclaim her, but even after three glasses of wine he could hear the note of caution still echoing in his head.

Donna refused help in the kitchen but did not begin to cook until ten o'clock. By then the wine had set in fully and Philip's head was throbbing. Dave had brought five pounds of fresh and bright coho, most of which burnt even after Carol pushed her way in and cheerfully insisted on "getting things going." They opened the front door to clear the smoke. When they finally sat down to dinner, Donna told them to wait while she lit candles. She lit the candles and then wobbled unsteadily toward the piano.

"Not again with that song," said Dave with a forced laugh. "Shoot the piano player, please." There was an uncomfortable silence and the room grew sullen.

"Leave her alone," Carol cut in. "She's just having fun."

Dave looked across the table at Adele. "What do you think of that song?" he asked her.

Adele pursed her lips thoughtfully before speaking. "I have heard it before," she said softly. "It is not my favorite."

Dave looked at her with a puzzled expression before busting out laughing. "Ha," he hooted. "Brilliant. Ha. Not my favorite. Catch that, Donna?"

"Fine then," said Donna, leaving the piano quiet and coming back to the table. "It's my house, but fine then."

"It's actually Edgar's house," said Dave, still grinning. He focused his attention back to Adele as everyone began to pick at their unpleasant food. "Where are you from anyway?"

Adele set her fork down. "I am from Fresno, California," she said.

"She's a Moonie, you know," said Donna, raising her wine glass and draining it. Then she enunciated precisely, "It is a cult."

"Jesus Christ, Donna," burst out Philip, pushing back from the table. "Jesus Christ, you are out of bounds." The small room seemed suddenly yawning and awful. Dave and Carol both looked down at their plates, wiping their mouths full of fish meat and pinbones. Adele sat unmoving, without a flicker of expression on her reddening face.

Donna leaned back in her chair and eyed Philip with a nonplussed expression. "I was just saying. I didn't mean anything by it." She patted the table. "Sit down and let's eat our dinner."

"Out of bounds," repeated Philip firmly.

Donna's face crumpled and tears welled in her eyes. "Oh fuck you, Philip. Just fuck you." She struggled up from the table, skewing the cloth, shaking the plates and wineglasses and ran up the stairs to the loft. Her sobbing filled the house.

Philip stood with his arms at his side, feeling the emptiness of shame heavy in his stomach. He looked around the table and saw three people staring down at their plates. "I'm sorry about all that," he mumbled lamely.

"Ah, hell," said Dave, dropping his napkin and standing. "It happens. Don't sweat it." He turned to Carol and put a tender hand on her shoulder. "We should be making a move though. Can't leave the babysitter there all night."

"Of course," said Philip, following them as they got their coats. "And sorry the salmon didn't turn out."

"Shit. Plenty of fish in the sea," said Dave. "A few pounds is nothing. I'll drop some more by and you guys can take another crack at it sometime." Philip nodded and smiled thinly. Carol called out a goodnight to Donna and left with Dave behind her.

Philip shut the door and turned to Adele, who was clearing the dishes. "I can do that," he said. Adele continued to gather the dishes. He stood next to her, blocking her way to the sink. "I'm sorry about all this," he said. "About everything. Let me get it. You can rest."

"I am not tired, Philip. I will finish this." She moved past him with a stack of plates.

"Phil?" Donna's voice came quavering from the loft. "Phil? I need you. I'm bleeding."

Philip turned. "What?" he called back.

"I'm bleeding. From my feet. I need you." The sobbing returned.

He reluctantly climbed the steps to the loft and switched on the lamp. Donna was hunched over in the bed, still wearing her clothes. Trickles of blood were coming from the arches of her feet, on the top of each midfoot, and there was a small amount of blood on her hands and the blankets. He knelt down beside the bed and looked at them. "Did you scrape your feet? Did you kick something?"

"No. Oh God."

"Just lie back. It's nothing, just scrapes. Let me get a bandage."

"Oh God," she moaned. "Oh Jesus."

He stepped quickly down the stairs, passing Adele in the kitchen, and went into the bathroom for the first-aid kit. He found some gauze and tape and ointment. He wet a rag in the sink and went back up to the loft.

"Here," he said, swabbing the rag on the scrapes. "Lie back."

"Oh God," she said, her face red with crying, her chapped lips stained with wine. "It's like stigmata. It hurts."

"Just lie back," he repeated. "You don't have. . . . It's nothing. This is from your new shoes. Probably just blisters and you scratched them. Stop freaking out."

She nodded, her head wobbling more than it should, and lay back on the pillow, letting Philip bandage her feet. Her breathing steadied. When he was done, he stood and moved beside her to turn off the lamp. She reached out and grabbed his arm.

"You were wrong," she said. "You were *defending* her. Her. A phony. You said she was strange, but over me, you were defending her."

"Go to sleep," he said.

She released his arm and rolled away from him. "You are the only man I've ever loved," she said.

Philip sat on the bed in the darkness for a time, listening to Donna's breath soften and become regular with sleep. He pulled the blankets up around her and then he stood and went downstairs.

Adele had finished in the kitchen and it was dark. By the glow of the Christmas bulbs and the dying fire he could see her silhouette on the couch. He moved quietly down the stairs and sat beside her. He sighed deeply and stared into the embers.

"When the True Father came to Alaska," she murmured after a time, "he said that God is interested in courageous people. God Himself is adventurous, and He also made us that way."

Philip slumped toward her, letting his head fall slowly into her lap. She moved her arm as he did so, placing her hand lightly on his side. "Let us not speak of it," he said. He felt her belly tighten in a stifled laugh.

"All right. But he also said that the salmon shall be the fish of the Moonies, that the salmon symbolizes the Moon spirit."

Philip tightened his belly, too, letting out a quiet snort. "It's all too much," he said.

"Yes."

They sat in silence, listening to the hiss and pop of the fire. Philip relaxed into Adele's lap, feeling the slow rise and fall of her breath move through her body.

"How are you on this island, Philip?" she asked softly.

He hesitated before answering, pushing thought aside. "I am stuck," he said finally, feeling as though the words would choke him. "I'm stuck in this little place and I can't move."

Adele sighed and moved her hand over his head, brushing his hair back over his ear with slow steady movements, again and again. "Every island longs for the continent," she whispered. The sound of her fingers on his scalp was like the sea, the breaking of waves. He rolled awkwardly onto his back and then again toward her, pressing his face into her belly and reaching an arm around her hips in an embrace. Adele did not move. She let him turn, stroking his back when he was settled. He pressed into her and nestled beneath her shirt. He kissed the skin of her stomach and pressed his cheek against its warmth. He pressed higher and she did not move. He felt her breast against his cheek and he kissed her softness once and then again. His lips found her nipple and he took it into his mouth. He tasted salt and the sound of the sea surged in his head and he felt the edges of his body obliterate into nothingness. Into oblivion and ecstasy. A vast quiet unlocked within him and filled him and surrounded him. Adele wrapped her arms around his body and held him close like that, to her.

From a great distance Philip heard a creak. Adele stiffened. Donna stood frozen on the middle stair, illuminated in the glow of the Christmas lights, the bandages on her feet stark and white. For a moment the world stopped. And then Donna coughed and turned slowly, quietly, back up the stairs.

acknowledgments

To get on in the world, one needs both luck and wits. As between the two, luck is more important. In the creation of this book, I've had plenty of luck – for which I am grateful and without which this book wouldn't exist. First off, I'm deeply thankful to the Iowa Writers' Workshop and the University of Iowa for the Iowa Arts Fellowship, which supported the initial writing of these stories. Thank you to Connie Brothers, Deb West, and Jan Zenisek for always steering me right.

I was extremely lucky in my teachers, especially Jim McPherson, Edward Carey, Kevin Brockmeier, and Scott Spencer, who taught me to fry bigger fish. Lan Samantha Chang was not only an inspiring teacher, but also an essential mentor and the most thoughtful reader of fiction I've encountered. I am forever grateful for her guidance and support. Of course, I also owe a debt of gratitude to all of my classmates at Iowa, for their patience, dedication, and good humor.

Many thanks to the University of Alaska Press, especially James Engelhardt, Krista West, and the editor of the Alaska Literary Series, Peggy Shumaker. Thanks also to Joeth Zucco, for her careful and thoughtful work with the manuscript, and to Kate Miles, for paving the way. Thanks also to Unity College, to my colleagues and students, for their inspiration and good will.

I've been luckiest of all in my family and pals. Many thanks to Chad Calease and Pete Wolf. Endless thanks to the Falcon, Cole, and O'Halloran families for their continued support and unflagging faith. Thanks to Mary and Asha. Thank you to my mother, Julie Van Driel, for surrounding me with books as a child. Thank you to my father, Spencer Falcon, for his always wise counsel. Most of all, thank you to my best friend and dearest love, Kacey Cole. Luck doesn't begin to describe it.

Zach Falcon's collection offers a masterful portrait of ordinary Alaskans as they find and lose themselves in this challenging but breathtaking northern landscape. These remarkable and haunting stories feature young children escaping to the woods as their family life unravels, down-and-out drifters forging unexpected bonds, and a stalled-out lawyer who can't quite make a decisive break from his stifling hometown. Falcon's extraordinary tales grab readers from the start. This isn't "fantasy Alaska," as one character puts it, but the real thing—a land of rusty tap water, isolated rain-soaked communities, and endless streams of cruise ship tourists set against a backdrop of spectacular natural beauty. *Cabin, Clearing, Forest* marks a stunning and unforgettable debut by an original new voice in Alaska literature.

—Susan Kollin, author of *Nature's State: Imagining Alaska as the Last Frontier*